GRAHAM J HOLMES WILSON was born in Melrose in the Scottish Borders. He attended St Mary's Prep School, where he was head boy, and is currently in his last year at Merchiston Castle School in Edinburgh. Aside from English, he also has a keen interest in history, the classics, rugby, journalism and acting. He hopes to go on to study Classical Civilisation at Exeter University next year. *The Ottoman Affair* is his first novel.

THE OTTOMAN AFFAIR

THE OTTOMAN AFFAIR

GRAHAM J HOLMES WILSON

ATHENA PRESS
LONDON

ISBN 978 1 84748 751 3

First published 2010 by
ATHENA PRESS
Queen's House, 2 Holly Road
Twickenham TW1 4EG
United Kingdom

Printed for Athena Press

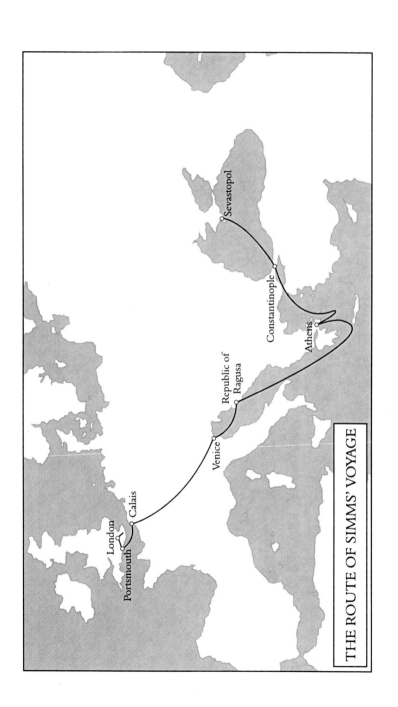

THE ROUTE OF SIMMS' VOYAGE

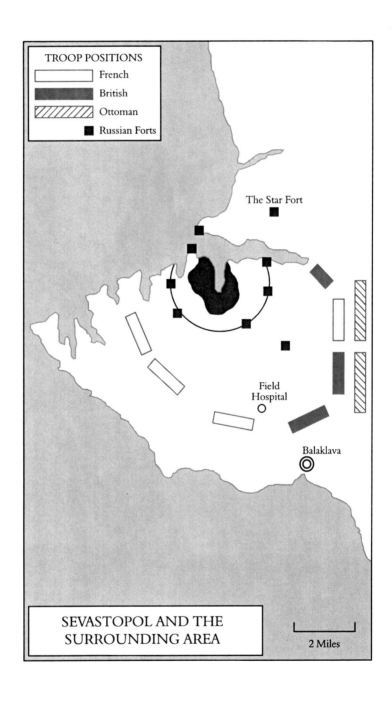

The Star Fort

Field
Hospital

Balaklava

SEVASTOPOL AND THE
SURROUNDING AREA

2 Miles

Contents

Part One

Venice, August 1855

Chapter One

As I gazed around the bustling square I caught a whiff of spice. It was an exotic scent of the unknown, hinting at mystery, floating across the water towards me from the ships unloading at the docks. All around, people hurried to and fro as the Italian sun beat down upon the entire scene, the stench of the docks and the citizens, and the unrelenting heat all adding yet another dimension to the many sensory encounters which I was experiencing. The sounds of the place enveloped me, whether it was the cries of the gondoliers hailing customers, the chattering of the old wives at the market or the soft swish of the sea and the cries of the gulls as they wheeled overhead.

I ventured through the crowd towards the shade of the Doge's Palace, seeking a refuge from the merciless sun (Englishmen are not made for Venetian summers), and played over in my mind the events of the last few months and the startling information I had had to digest. It had been a clear morning in late June and I had recently returned from Russia after visiting my brother there. It had been a tough few weeks and I thought it would be best to recuperate before rejoining my regiment (shortly due to travel out to the Crimea). And so it followed that I embarked on a few weeks of lazing about in the gardens, clubs and billiard rooms of Kent (operating from Oakam, Father's stately pile in the country) and rooms in London. Needless to say, there was a great deal of celebrating to be done, for it is not every day that one is promoted to the rank of captain, and particularly at the young age of twenty-four! Bearing this in mind, I set off on a mission to visit as many of my old school and university friends that I could find.

I was finally able to make use of my membership at Boodle's[1], and it proved a useful base from which to experience the delights of the town. I took up rooms in London, Grosvenor Place in fact

---

[1] A popular and distinguished St James's club.

– a rather plush set of apartments that Father was kind enough to put me up in. It was a tough job persuading the old boy, but the family's townhouse is just so out of the way and in any case it was currently being rented out to another gentleman, a Mr John Sykes. Now that I had returned to the social circle of England and London from the chilly wastes of the Russian Empire, my friends somehow took this as a sign that I had been deprived of all entertainment, fun, conversation and even just basic human company. In order to rectify this I was subjugated to a constant torrent of balls, hunts, shoots, dinner parties, trips to the theatre and just plain, good old evenings of indulgence with old drinking companions from King's.

And so it was that I passed the next few weeks in a sociable haze – and in some cases a rather intimate one; it always amazes me just how much of an act the whole female sex put on today of being delicate, innocent and shy (as this is what they most certainly are not; indeed the words 'boisterous', 'malicious' and 'extremely amiable' spring to mind). Thus my resting time was free of distractions, or at least all but one.

It began as I was settling down to my breakfast on the terrace. I was back at Oakam – running out of funds for the month is always such a depressing occurrence! – on a particularly fine morning when Bradley appeared with a letter upon his tray that was addressed to me and marked to be of the utmost importance. It transpired that I had received a summons to the Foreign Office! Puzzled, but at the same time intrigued, I told Bradley to make ready the carriage and so made my way to London.

Upon my arrival, my hopes of pursuing other plans that day were shattered when I called in on the Office. Much to my dismay, London was being simply lashed with rain, and it was with trepidation that I bailed out of my carriage, hurrying across the cobbles and up the steps. Bradley's pathetic attempt to keep me dry and cover me from the torrent with his umbrella had failed utterly, and I stood for a moment in the foyer, dripping, earning me a stern gaze of disapproval from a clerk.

A tall fellow approached, peering down at me from his bony nose and haughtily inquired if I was 'that fellow Simms'. I replied that Captain Simms was here, and was damned confused about this whole business. At that the chap whipped around, barking out a sharp 'Follow me!' and sped off up a nearby staircase.

I told Bradley to remain where he was until I returned and set off in pursuit. We wound our way along a maze of corridors and staircases, an endless procession of doors and offices until we finally came to a halt, stopping outside a panelled oak door. Without another word, he swung the door open and indicated that I was to enter. As soon as I had gone in he shut the door, leaving me completely clueless as to what was to happen. And so it was that I turned around to face a man hunched down over a bureau. He looked familiar, and I was sure we had met before. He was a well-known figure, someone in authority, frequently in the papers. Suddenly it came to me. It was none other than the Foreign Minister! Surprised, it took me a moment to adjust.

He glanced up from some papers on his desk and looked me up and down, taking in everything about my appearance. 'Simms,' he said, finally, peering down at me, 'how do you do?'

I replied, and returned the inquiry, which he ignored.

'I have no time for pleasantries, Simms, time is precious and unfortunately it's something I have very little of. You might as well take a seat and I'll explain this whole sticky business.'

By now my curiosity was intense and so I took a seat, desperate to find out what it was that had disturbed me from the last few days of my leave.

'No doubt you have been following the war in the Crimea,' the Minister began, 'and know of the fragile state of things in that region. The entire thing is a great big mess, especially since that fool Cardigan had got involved.[2] It's one thing losing a company, but your entire brigade! Madness! Anyhow, we have recently heard that things could get considerably worse. As you may know, Britain's relations with the Ottomans have never been particularly friendly; indeed, this alliance is merely a convenience for both sides, and everyone knows it. However, as far as the British

---

[2] James Thomas Brudenell, the 7th Earl of Cardigan. The Earl led the disastrous Charge of the Light Brigade at the Battle of Balaklava. He was portrayed in mixed lights, but was usually seen as either incompetent or heroic, depending on how romantic or cynical the critic was. Either way, the Charge of the Light Brigade is seen as certainly one of the greatest and most dramatic tactical blunders in the Crimean War, and possibly in the entirety of British military history.

command in Crimea is concerned, the Turks are friends – something that could be proved to be very, very wrong if what we're dealing with is true.' He paused, looking at me with that severe stare of his, and continued his tale.

'A few weeks ago we received word from our man in Venice that a Turkish navy captain, a certain Ibrahim Quatal, had arrived, bringing with him a rumour about some very unusual papers. The story, as he had heard it, was that these documents contained plans for a Turkish attack aimed at British protected lands in the Crimea. It seems that the Turks do not believe that we'll go quietly when this whole infernal business is over – although God knows why; it's bad enough having to blow that bloody peninsula up, let alone having to look after it. It seems that Quatal had been ordered to transport an Ottoman general and his staff from Istanbul. These men were to carry the papers. However, while crossing the Black Sea they were attacked by the Russian Navy. The general and his staff perished, indeed the ship itself sunk, while Quatal and a few of his crew made off in a lifeboat. While executing his own order to abandon ship, Quatal came across the fallen general and found him clutching a leather bag, obviously containing something he was willing to give his life to protect. The captain took it, assuming it was important, and thus valuable.

'For a night and a day the Turks were marooned in their boat, and nothing could distract the captain from seeing what was inside the bag. Eventually he gave into his curiosity and tipped the contents onto his lap. What he saw amazed him. At first he was terrified; he knew that to possess that kind of knowledge was dangerous, but through his panic he saw a fabulous opportunity. No one knew that he had taken the documents; as far as the Sultan was concerned they had perished with the ship. If Quatal could find the right buyer he would be a rich man, rich enough to leave the navy and buy his way into Ottoman society. He kept the nature of the documents from his crew, and by the time they had been picked up and returned to Istanbul he was the only one who still remembered the mysterious leather bag he had snatched from the dead general.

'Quatal journeyed to Venice, a city famed for its reputation as an international hub, where he hoped he could find a buyer, hopefully the British or French. Our man, hearing the story, immediately arranged a meeting with Quatal. We received correspondence from Burnes two weeks ago, and have heard nothing from him since. Three days ago we gained a note from Venice that had been hastily sent by Burnes' secretary, telling us of how he has gone missing, and it seems Quatal has fled to Istanbul, or so we think. The man was obviously scared and not in a fit state to investigate. Thanks to this war with the Russians, we are understaffed to say the least, which leaves us with no one to look into this. I have heard about your exploits in April with the Russians and I must admit I was impressed. A mere lieutenant saving the Queen's Envoy to the Tsar! Splendid! Congratulations on your promotion. Indeed, when I read your story in *The Times* I was struck, and the first thing I though was, If there was ever a resourceful chap, then it's this Simms fellow…'

The Minister was of course referring to my adventure two months ago. While visiting my brother in St Petersburg a spate of anti-British sentiment had sprung up, probably based on our attempted assault in the Baltic and siege of Sevastopol, resulting in an assassination attempt on the Envoy. Indeed, I had come to warn my younger half-brother Richard of the danger and accompany him home, a point to which he had consented, but we were not to be let off without a fight. The Russian public, the serf or peasant class that make up the bulk of the population, had been stirred up by some local madman. Inspired by this fellow's ranting, they attacked the Envoy's house with stones and torches. Although the Envoy's staff had lost their wits, Richard and I kept a cool head and were able to escape with the Envoy to the docks, where we secured passage to Stockholm and back to Harwich.

The Envoy had been exceptionally grateful and had mentioned Edward and me in the highest manner, resulting in a speedy advancement for us in our respective fields: myself a captain now, and Richard an assistant to the Ambassador to Spain. The Envoy also made a gift of several excellent bottles of cognac, unfortunately most of which have gone by now (the family and associates made a great fuss of the promotion, as they do of anything, and father will look for any excuse for a celebration). It had been a tender few days after my return, to say the least.

'So, Simms,' said the Minister, jerking my train of though back to the present, 'it seems you have a mind for these things. You seem to be sensible enough, brave in the right quantities (as Balaklava had proved there is such a thing as being too brave) and have a gift for languages, or so your masters at Cambridge claim.'

Indeed this was true; I had studied French, German and Italian at King's before joining the army two years ago, and I had left college with full colours, although I had had little opportunity to practise my skills in recent years.

He continued, 'I don't know if you have heard the real reports from the Crimea but in case you haven't, I'll tell you. That peninsula is hell itself: the mud, the death, the disease, the entire thing is a damned mess. The Foreign Office is offering you a chance to escape from that. Right now you won't find adventure in the army, you'll find mud, fools and a coffin. What we can give you is adventure, in the real sense of the word. We want you to find out what really happened to Burnes, and if not, to secure those papers. So what will it be? The cold and sludge of Sevastopol, or the sun and spice of Venice?'

Truth be told, the Crimea had never really appealed to me, and so after a moment's hesitation I gave my consent. I was now the Minister's man, an agent of the Foreign Office.

'Don't worry,' the Minister said, 'I will see to it that you will retain your commission, and you will stay on full pay, as well as receiving, if your mission if successful, a small reward from Her Majesty's Government. I must say I am glad you've accepted; you seem like a good man with a sharp mind and it would have grieved me to hear of your death by the Russians.'

The Minister rose, and as he passed through the doorway turned and looked straight at me, 'I expect great things in the future from you, Captain Simms, great things. Don't fail me!' And with that he was gone.

His adjutants had left with him, leaving me alone, seated in that bare room. I rose and made my way through the corridors, all the while surrounded by the sound of diplomacy. After a while of tramping round I was able to finally find the exit from the damned place, only to be held up at the very moment of my escape by a ratty little man with a droopy moustache.

'Captain Simms, sir!' he cried. 'Thank heavens I caught you. I have your orders here. Your passage leaves from Portsmouth to Calais on the third.'

I was surprised. The third was no more than two days away.

He carried on. 'From there you can take the post wagons to Venice. I have a letter here from the Minister containing all the details. Best of luck to you, Simms.' And with that he abruptly turned and strode off, leaving me in the doorway clutching the paper he had thrust into my hand.

With the help of Bradley, my manservant, I was able to pack up my belongings and get myself to Portsmouth. Of course the family were delighted and somewhat relieved. My mother and sisters had worried in a way only mothers and sisters can about the danger of the war in the Crimea; indeed the task I had been set seemed a heavenly reprieve, and an honourable one at that. And so it was with excited trepidation that I left my family once more and arrived at the dour port on the south coast.

Chapter Two

My journey to Venice was not exciting. The weather in Calais was abysmal and the crossing rough, as were the roads. It took us a week to reach Piedmont and the Northern Duchies as we journeyed south and then east to the city of the Doges.

Venice was a place I had only heard about, but as is not the case in many examples, Venice lived up to the magnificent descriptions that had been made of it. My first view of it was from the west at night, and it seemed to me like a glittering jewel, hovering over the Adriatic, the light of a thousand candles flickering in the soft breeze that blew in from the ocean. By the time we reached the city, dawn was unfurling her golden tresses across the town, illuminating the magnificence of the decaying palazzos and piazzas. And so it was that after a day's rest I had decided to venture out in the centre of town in the freshness of the morning, and begin my quest to unravel the skein of mystery and intrigue that hung over the city like a rich and complex smog.

Once in the shade of the palace, I reached into my suit pocket for a cheroot, with which I puffed up my own rich and complex smog around me, while I contemplated the events which this city had borne witness to. A bearded man to my left looked on disapprovingly. There was only one place to start as I could see it, and that was to interview Burnes' secretary – a Richard Hewitt, if the Minister's letter spoke true. According to the letter, Burnes' rooms had not been far from here, and so I ventured into the sunshine of the square for a brief moment before I stepped into the cool, enveloping gloom of the alleys and canals.

After a short walk I arrived at the palazzo. As with many buildings in Venice, there was an air of grand decay about the place. The paint was peeling on the shutters and it sat squatly, in the shadow of a larger house across the street, although that wasn't in much of a better condition either. The stench of the canal drifted past me, despite the fine aroma of my still smouldering cheroot. I took a last puff before tossing the thing away and watched a final plume of smoke wind its way up through the thick air before I ground my boot over it, extinguishing the glowing tobacco. Turning to the gloomy portal, I knocked, the noise echoing throughout the place, suggesting a spacious interior.

After around half a minute I heard footsteps and the sliding of a bolt, and was suddenly faced with a pair of intelligent and startlingly blue eyes. The servant introduced himself as Gino and inquired as to my business. I told him to notify Hewitt that Simms, the Minister's agent, was here and would see if he would talk with him. Gino reappeared after a minute or so and ushered me in, bowing and offering his hand for my hat, which I surrendered. As it is with quite a few of the palazzos in Venice, the interior of the house could hardly be compared to the exterior. A chequered black and white marble floor lay beneath a spacious entrance hall, and through a doorway ahead of me I could see a pleasant and sunny garden in a courtyard. Above me the clear sky was glazed an azure blue, the hidden sun illuminating a three-storey courtyard in a pleasant white stone. A cloistered walkway opened onto the courtyard on the first two levels, but on the third there was a blank stone wall, punctuated only by wooden shutters, none of which were open.

It seemed to be a well-kept place, and it seemed that Burnes must have been a man of quite some means. I also happened to notice a young lady who was reclining upon a white stone bench, taking the air in the garden. She was clothed in white, and was wearing one of those wide-brimmed hats that were so in fashion this season to keep the sun off her pale features. I surveyed her from a distance. She was young, of good shape, and was blessed with noble, distinguishing features; altogether a beautiful woman. As she caught sight of me and locked eyes I was distracted by Gino offering refreshment, but I declined. Ten o'clock in the morning was hardly the time for the first brandy, particularly in the presence of a lady.

Gino hurried off to fetch Hewitt and I was left alone with the young woman. I always have despised the excessive formality that has come to curse relations in England, and so I figured that as we were in Italy, and I was pursuing an official investigation of the highest importance, I should acquaint myself with this charming young lady as soon as possible. Obviously she was thinking the same thing, as she flashed me a coy smile, parting her full red lips to reveal a dainty row of pearly teeth, and, just for a flicker of a second, her small, delicate tongue darting out playfully, wetting and caressing the scarlet lips that encased it.

Yes, I concluded, an acquaintance was very much necessary. I approached and halted before her, dipping my head down, and accepting the proffered hand, grazing it briefly with my mouth. Then, looking up at her with the most rakish smile I could pull off, I said to her, 'Captain Henry Simms, ma'am, most definitely at your service…'

I lingered there for a few seconds, watching as she blushed gently, which had a most pleasing effect, looked flustered for a few more, which again was most flattering, before composing herself, and declaring in the most proper manner she could, 'What a pleasure it is to finally find a gentleman in this city, Captain. I am Miss Burnes. With such manners as you have displayed, I may find myself having to make use of your services.'

Again that hint of a smile flickered across her dainty features in what can only be described as a most enticing manner. This pleasant interlude was, however, unfortunately disturbed by a bustling movement coming from behind me, and I turned round to face the source, vowing to make sure I continued this line of inquiry later on. I stepped away from Miss Burnes before the cause of the noise entered the courtyard and, clasping my hands behind my back, awaited whoever it was that was coming.

A man who could only be Hewitt was puffing his way towards me; indeed the fellow was anything but slim, and his face was red with the heat and exertion. He was middle-aged and had a nervous air about him. He kept on patting his forehead with a large handkerchief and had a face etched with worry. His hair was thinning, scraped across his glistening pate in a last-ditch attempt to hold back the onslaught of baldness. He heaved his bulk towards me, extended a chubby hand and gasped, 'Captain Simms, so very glad to meet you. I'm Arthur Hewitt, as I'm sure you know. It's been a most terrible business, most terrible indeed. How can I help you?'

During this introduction, I had followed him over to another stone bench nearby, carved in the likeness of two of those winged lions the Venetians are so fond of, holding up a block of grooved stone. We sat down, the young lady eying Hewitt with an expression of mild derision and distaste.

'Oh, forgive me! Allow me to introduce Miss Isabella Burnes, niece of Mr Burnes. Miss Burnes, Captain Simms...'

'A pleasure, ma'am. Once again!' This earned a wry smile from the girl, and a bemused look from Hewitt, who I suppose was now her chaperone. I added, 'I hope that we may come to know each other well in the coming weeks, while I investigate the chilling disappearance of your uncle.'

She cocked her head slightly in acknowledgement. 'It is always pleasing to know that the utmost is being done to pursue this most horrid of matters, Captain Simms. As for your wish, well, hope is a fickle thing, Captain, and who knows what may come of fickle things?'

Again I caught a flicker of playfulness in those deep eyes, while that entrancing smile danced around her mouth for a third and final time.

Hewitt coughed and, giving Miss Burnes a most unsubtle and very meaningful glance, proceeded with his original line.

'The disappearance of Mr Burnes has shocked all of us, especially me. I had no idea where to turn to here in Venice; indeed, the entire city holds fear for me now. I really had no option but to ask for help from London. I mean, I am hardly in a fit state to do much investigating myself – I am reduced to a bundle of nerves!'

As you have no doubt gathered by now, Hewitt was a coward of the highest degree. He seemed more concerned about his own life being in danger than the disappearance of his superior and a high-ranking Foreign Office official! I won't bother including the whole of the conversation, as his talk was dreary and repetitive, continuing much along the same lines as I have described above. Of far more interest was Miss Burnes, who, although she did not speak, remained throughout the entire conversation, providing a welcome distraction from Hewitt's wittering.

I was, however, able to glean some useful information from the exchange. I was able to learn from Hewitt the place where Burnes had arranged to meet Quatal, and what Burnes looked like should I find him. It seemed he was a tall, powerful man; a Scotsman, with black hair, bushy eyebrows and whiskers than came down over his cheeks as well as a fine set of mustachios. He was a well-known and friendly man who was well connected with all the British families in Venice. It also transpired that Gino, the doorman, was actually Burnes' manservant, and Hewitt offered Gino's services to me as a guide in the unfriendly city. This seemed wise advice. Who better to help me find Burnes than his Venetian manservant?

After a while, however, I had finally had enough of Hewitt, although I was intrigued by Miss Burnes. She was certainly a delightful specimen, with a forwardness that one can only ever find in Englishwomen away from home. I would most definitely have to make sure I ran into her again. However, something was not quite right about her. It was only later on when thinking about the exchange that I realised she seemed strangely unconcerned about her uncle. Still, maybe Burnes had been one of those rather unpleasant uncles who are always the focus of those Gothic novels that women are so obsessed with... Besides, it seemed that the attention that she should have been giving Burnes had been turned on me, and who was I to complain? All the same, matters were pressing, and so far I had achieved little in Venice, so I regretfully took my leave, taking Gino with me.

We passed through the looming doorway and were brought out again into the gloomy alley, momentarily oblivious to our surroundings due to the bright sunshine that we had experienced in the courtyard. After a few seconds we were able to carry on, although the question was, where should we carry on to? Hewitt had given me a slip of paper with the address where Burnes was meant to meet his contact – a tavern it seemed, deep within the city. I turned to Gino and showed him the address and ordered him in Italian to lead me there, a tactic that instantly gained me favour in the servant's eyes.

And so it was that we set off, dragged deeper and deeper into the city. All the while the alleys grew closed together, the houses seemed to loom over us, the canals grew murkier and the inhabitants grew more and more gloomy and suspicious looking.

After a while, Gino turned around and asked if I'd thought to bring some protection, as the area we were approaching was rough and the inhabitants would surely take an interest in my expensive clothes. I replied in the affirmative and nervously checked the pair of pistols that I had hidden under my jacket.

We proceeded carefully from that point onwards, not looking the locals in the eye and moving quickly. After a brief moment we stopped at a point where two canals met. Across a small bridge there was a dingy-looking place which Gino identified as the tavern. It seemed a strange place for a British agent to meet, and the entire locality had more than a hint of skulduggery about it. Nonetheless, I had a mission to complete, so we pressed on and entered.

The tavern itself was a seedy place, little more than an ale-house for the poor. The fat landlord stared at us as we entered, making it pointedly obvious we were not welcome. However I had no option but to question him. I asked him if he had seen a Turk or a man fitting Burnes' description recently but he had no information for me. I looked around at the customers, and was surprised to see the bearded man I had seen in the square. Taking little notice of it, I took in the other patrons. A dark man with his hood over his eyes sat hunched in the corner, deep in conversation with a few fellows: Turks. This seemed promising, and so I made my way over, despite Gino's quiet cautions. I approached them and addressed them in Italian, asking them if they would happen to know of a certain Captain Quatal.

At that point the table went silent and slowly all but the cloaked man turned and stared. I was also aware that, rather interestingly, the bearded man had my attention as well. Nothing was said for a good ten seconds, so I repeated my question. Once again I was met with silence; by now the whole tavern had turned to see what was happening. I felt Gino by my side, urging me to caution and to leave now, and so it was that I turned and left, receiving a curious glance from the bearded man as I made my way out.

It was only when we had turned the corner and gone a

considerable distance that I realised we were being followed. All at once Gino turned around and I must admit I feared the worse, thinking perhaps it was the cloaked man and his Turks. However, it was actually the bearded man from the tavern. I decided enough was enough – I had to find out who he was. To my surprise he did not slip away as soon as we approached, but rather he stood his ground and awaited us, head bowed. I took the opportunity to study him. He was of medium height, with broad shoulders and a long beard tucked into his belt. What I could see of his face was tanned and covered in deep lines. He wore a stern expression, though not cruel or dishonest, although as we all know appearances can be deceptive. He raised his head as we grew nearer and a smell of sweat and incense drifted towards us, the former unfortunately being the prevalent scent. His eyes were hazel and were sunk deep into his craggy and worn face, surrounded by the thatch of his grey stringy hair than hung down under his felt cap. He raised a hand in greeting and stepped towards us. I felt for the stock of my pistol, reassured by the feel of the polished wood on my palm.

'There will be no need for violence, Captain,' he grumbled, taking me by surprise. How did he know my rank? He carried on, his deep, gravelly voice, although quiet, carrying clearly towards us. 'I believe we seek the same man, the Captain Quatal you asked for. You won't find him; he left quite some time ago. Indeed, I am due to leave soon.'

This was an interesting new development, a third party; could this man be after the papers too?

'May I inquire as to who exactly you are? And why have you been following me?' I asked, still feeling shaken as to how he knew my business.

'I am Brivopolis, Father Brivopolis of the Greek Orthodox Church and a humble servant of His Majesty King Otto of Greece. And you are Captain Henry Simms, until recently Lieutenant Simms, of Her Majesty's Government in London – if I am not mistaken?'

To say the least I was amazed and managed to spit out a confirmation of the information he had presented me with.

He carried on, 'I have been sent by His Majesty's court to find

Captain Quatal and his infamous papers, the same reason you are here, I think?'

'Yes,' I replied, 'but also no. Not long ago a senior British official, a Mr Burnes, made contact with Quatal, looking to acquire the documents you mentioned. They were meant to meet in that tavern, only Burnes never made it there, and if what you say is true, Quatal has fled, leaving me at a loss as to how to proceed.'

'Now this is an interesting development,' the priest said. 'I met a Kyrios Burnes two weeks ago, if I remember rightly. We had both been trying to contact Quatal. He had been quite the competitor, desperate to secure the papers for Britain, and I was surprised when he had seemingly pulled out of the race. I had thought my mission was successful. With the British out of the running I would have no problem in gaining the papers for Greece, but I was not planning for Quatal to flee within the next few days. Your news would explain this; it was a puzzling mystery at first.' He paused.

'I say we join forces,' he went on, 'and together both our countries can split the spoils of our work. If what I hear is true then Quatal left for Istanbul, seeking safety in his home country. What say you to continuing the chase to Turkey?'

This was an interesting proposition. It would mean that I would be considerably less safe than I was in Venice, but the mission must be completed. However, I had always expressed a deep desire to explore the East. I pondered over it at length, running through in my mind all the different consequences. It would mean that the search for Burnes would have to be left again to Hewitt, who was not a character I placed much trust in, and I would have to give up the opportunity to ingratiate myself with Burnes' niece. However, if Burnes had met Quatal, and Quatal was in Istanbul, then by following him surely I would reach both Burnes and the papers.

Consoled by this thought, I gave my consent and instructed him that we should leave in three days. I gave him the address of my palazzo and was about to leave when I was suddenly aware that we were being watched. I started towards the observer, one of the Turks from the tavern, who was hidden behind a couple of barrels at the end of the alley. He upped and turned to leave, but I wasn't about to let him off lightly – there was something that was not right about those Ottomans. I started in pursuit and he bolted, rushing off down the street, bowling over an old fish seller. I sprinted off after him, leaping over the piles of fish scattered over the flags.

I reached inside my jacket, grasping for my pistol, which I levelled and fired off, cracking a tile above my quarry's head. I let loose an oath and continued my chase. He sped round the corner, and I followed, hot on his heels. Cries of alarm were going up on either side of us as alarmed citizens leapt out of our path.

Suddenly he darted into a side doorway, catching me off guard. I followed and found myself in a courtyard very like the one at Burnes' place, but with a stair running up the inside of the garden to the top floors.

At first I was at a loss as to where the Turk had gone but then I caught him, speeding up the steps. I spurred myself on and darted after him, thinking that I would have him cornered.

Unfortunately I was to be proved wrong. He nipped through the open doorway at the top of the stairs and was lost to my view in the corridor up there. I paused briefly at the doorway and reached for my still loaded pistol and then proceeded carefully; he could be lurking in any one of the side rooms ready to burst out on me. I heard a shuffling in one of them and stopped outside, catching my breath and then bursting in.

He was standing in the windowsill, hunched up. I pointed my pistol, more to threaten than to harm – I wanted him alive to question. He opened his mouth to reveal rows of small, white sharp teeth arrayed in a smile, chuckled and leapt.

I cried out and rushed to the sill, looking for a sign of him. To my amazement he had cleared the street and was on the next building. By the time I had clambered up into the window he was long gone, leaping and running across the tiled rooftops. It was no use, and so I turned and slipped my pistol back under my coat, disappointed and exhausted, and came back out onto the stairs and into the sunlight.

Who was my mysterious watcher – a friend of Quatal's? Did he have knowledge of Burnes? Whoever he was, he obviously was not friendly; the looks I received from him and his cohorts in the bar were not welcoming. The hooded figure was someone I would have to find out more about, as I was sure he had something to do with Burnes' disappearance.

By the time I had returned to the alley where I had talked with Brivopolis, he was gone, although Gino had waited faithfully for me and was relieved to hear me ask him to escort me back to my palazzo. I turned over the events of the day and the offer Brivopolis had made me. It had been a truly remarkable morning, truly remarkable. I elected to return to the house, freshen up, have a light spot of lunch and pursue the matter with Bradley in the afternoon after I had recuperated.

It took us just over half an hour to return home and I bade Gino farewell as I pushed open the door of the rented palazzo. I was greeted with a cheerful halloo from Bradley, which I returned. I watched his eyes widen as I spilled forth my account of my adventurous morning and appeared speechless for a few moments before enquiring, 'But sir, are you sure we can trust this Brivopolis chap? I mean he seems mighty shady, if you catch my drift.'

'George,' I said, addressing him by his Christian name, 'he claimed to be a priest, and a servant of the Greek Royal Court. At any rate his countenance was that of a trustworthy man. I think he is who he says he is but you are right, we must take caution, and it is probably worth keeping an eye on the fellow if you can spare one. In any case he is a lead, and we need any lead we can get if we are to complete our task. Anyway, time for a spot of lunch, but I think I will refresh myself upstairs before we eat. See to it that the cook prepares something, if you please.'

I made my way up the marble staircase that graced the central hall and turned down the corridor leading to my rooms. I entered the bedroom and stripped off my jacket, crossing over to admire the view over the city before closing the shutters. I thought to splash some water over my face to sharpen my mind for what was to come and moved towards the bathroom, bustling towards the sink. My mind flickered back and forth, thinking first about the chase, that mysterious fellow, and then back to the alluring Miss Burnes, whose sparkling charm had definitely touched a nerve. It was only when I looked at my reflection that I realised there wasn't something quite right about the room; something was watching from behind me. I slowly turned around, finger on my pistols, which I had luckily kept with me, to face my unknown assailant. The next few moments are something that will live with me for the rest of my life.

I had found Burnes.

Chapter Three

They had hung him from my bathroom roof and left him to swing round slowly until his blank eyes stared into mine. I stood, paralysed by shock for several minutes, my heart pounding, until finally reason returned to me. I gave a cry for Bradley, shouting for him to come quick. I was left to face the grisly silence in the room while I heard Bradley running upstairs, listening until he burst breathless into the bedroom.

'In here, Bradley. I recommend you steel yourself.'

'But why sir, what could be—' his words were cut short as he encountered the cadaver. 'Wrong,' he finished, flabbergasted by what he saw. 'Is that... Mr Burnes, sir?'

'I believe so. At any rate, it fits Hewitt's description.' It seemed he had been strangled, as large red fingermarks adorned his throat; however, I was unable to examine his head without feeling a wave of nausea coming on. My eyes fell to his hands and I noticed something clutched in his left; a note perhaps? A note it was, which I had to prise from his cold fingers, a gruesome experience I assure you. It was addressed to me, something which intensely worried me. So much for the Minister's reassurance that Venice was safer than the Crimea. Would I be the murderer's next target?

I decided that we would have to leave Venice earlier than planned. I sent a runner to Hewitt to inform him of the news, and another one to the tavern I had been to that day to find where Brivopolis lodged. I couldn't bear the sight of that ghastly corpse, so I called for one of the servants to cut it down. I gagged while they carried it out of the room. While I waited for Hewitt and the Greek to arrive I busied myself with packing and recommended Bradley to do the same. Before long we had our personal possessions together and I settled down in the salon on the bottom floor while Bradley applied himself to some menial task.

After two hours, and the last of the Envoy's cognac, the two men finally answered my summons, bursting in and asking to hear what news was so dreadful it had disturbed them from their afternoon rest. Their tempers flared up once I had told them what was afoot, with Hewitt uttering exclamations of panic and shock; indeed at one point I thought the pathetic man was going to swoon. Brivopolis accepted Burnes' death more calmly, but he failed to hide the gleam of fear which occupied his eyes. While Hewitt expostulated to himself, Brivopolis and I planned what our next move would be.

'Well, there's only one course of action we can take as I see it,' I began. 'We must find Quatal; it seems that damn Mussulman holds all the answers.' Brivopolis looked at me cautiously from beneath his dark brows. 'Of course you are right, but do you feel it is wise to follow him to Constantinople? If our lives are at risk here, only God knows what danger we shall be in if we leave for that city!'

I surveyed him, pondering his response, but I knew that I had to have answers, and it seemed that these answers were all in one place: Constantinople. 'We cannot give up the hunt now. You know just as well as I do the importance of those papers. To abandon the chase is to abandon all our honour as well. I hardly think your German[3] would be too happy if you were to return with empty pockets...' The Greek bridled at these words but could not find a suitable response. In the end he mumbled his consent and turned away to engage Hewitt.

And so it was settled. Bradley and I were to go to Constantinople, jewel in the crown of the Ottomans, with its alluring and exotic taste of the Orient, filled with mystery, corruption, murder and mosques, that lay on the deep waters of the Bosphorus, revered prize of Constantine, Justinian and Suleiman[4] and

---

[3] The German that Simms refers to here is the German King of Greece, Otto I.

[4] The Roman Emperor Constantine, who renamed Byzantium Constantinople in his honour, made the city into a capital of the Western Empire. Suleiman the Magnificent, an Ottoman sultan, prized the city above all others, and went about making it into the architectural capital of the Empire, commissioning buildings such as the famous Blue Mosque. Justinian I was one of the greatest Byzantine emperors, constructing both the Justinian Wall around the city and the celebrated Haghia Sophia, originally a church before the Ottomans converted it into a mosque.

countless others. I remember as a boy listening to my masters' lessons on the great Byzantine Emperors, hearing tales of the campaigns of Nikephorus and John against the barbaric Turks of Rum, enveloping myself completely in dreams of the plot and intrigue of the East and of the mighty hordes assailing Anatolia and Nicaea, and finally Constantinople itself. However, suddenly the thought came to me that I would have to put my plans involving Miss Burnes on hold until I returned. This put rather a dark cloud over things, but I suppose you can't win every time. Anyway, if our mission were to succeed, I would be a hero of the empire, and that is something that always goes down well in the eyes of delightful young ladies...

Hewitt by this point had turned to Brivopolis, suspiciously eying up the Greek. I suddenly became aware that the two had yet to be introduced. 'Hewitt, allow me to introduce Father Brivopolis, servant of the Greek Orthodox Church and King Otto I of Greece. Have no worries, his interests are similar to ours and he can be trusted.'

Hewitt dabbed his glistening forehead with a handkerchief, extended a sweaty hand and stuttered out, 'Delighted, of course, how do you do, sir.' But before Brivopolis could give him an answer he started mewing pathetically, 'Of course, Simms, one of us must stay, hold the fort if you see what I mean, keep in touch with the authorities in London. After all,' he concluded, somehow managing to rustle up some pride from somewhere, 'I am technically holding Mr Burnes' position, and it would be disobeying orders if were to accompany you to Constantinople – abandoning my post, if you see what I mean.'

Brivopolis and I exchanged glances, and he smiled wryly. 'Of course you must stay, Hewitt,' I began. 'For us to succeed we must be sure our backs are guarded. I can think of no one braver to hold our position in Venice. After all, someone has to inform the Foreign Office of our change in plans, and who better than you, the most experienced diplomat of the three of us?'

He perked up at these words, muttering, 'Well of course, well put, as you said... diplomatic training, of course.'

I continued, 'Since Brivopolis and I must prepare for departure, would you be so kind as to use your contacts here to secure us safe passage? It will be an early start, so I recommend we start organising ourselves now. So, I think it's back to the palazzo with you, Hewitt, and Brivopolis and I will begin our preparations.'

Hewitt positively beamed at me, so great was his relief to be spared the journey. I couldn't help muttering under my breath, 'Damn coward!' as he turned his back. Luckily only Brivopolis heard, producing another of his tight smiles, and we watched as Hewitt set off out the front door and down the street accompanied by his manservant.

Brivopolis turned towards me, his beard waggling as he spoke. 'Is Mr Hewitt to be trusted? He doesn't exactly seem as if he is one we can rely on.'

I answered, 'To say that Arthur Hewitt is a coward is an understatement, but he is a useful coward. He can use his embassy contacts to help us, and I'd rather have him here than holding us up in Constantinople. Anyway, what's done is done; will you stay for a drink?'

'No thank you, I feel that an early night is in order after tonight's events, and we will be in need of all our faculties in the morning. Today has been busy enough without us needlessly lengthening it; I'm afraid I must bid you a goodnight. Shall I call upon you first tomorrow, or shall I meet you at the docks?'

'I think here is best. Very well, good night to you, sir, I look forward to seeing you in the morning.'

I escorted him to the door and sent him off to his lodgings with a male servant. As for myself, I returned to the drawing room, lit up a cheroot and pondered the events of the day. I turned them over in my mind, gazing at the smouldering leaf, before retiring to bed. Tomorrow would hold many challenges.

Chapter Four

I stirred and groaned, swatting away the object on my shoulder, only to my utmost annoyance to have it return. I soon identified the object to be Bradley's hand, shaking me from my pleasant slumber. 'What the devil do you want, Bradley?' I grumbled sleepily, peering up at him from my bed as he shuffled over to the window and opened the curtains. Dawn was yet to break and a dull grey seeped through the panes, barely illuminating the room. Bradley stood silhouetted against the twilight before turning.

'Mr Brivopolis is here, sir, and he's waiting in the drawing room. I've supplied him with some coffee, and I've got the remainder here,' he said, waggling a silver coffee pot in my direction.

'Very well, Bradley. Pour me a cup while I make myself ready.'

I heaved myself out of bed and trudged to the bathroom, halting at the door, suddenly remembering the events of the previous day. 'Actually I think I shall use the guest bathroom today, Bradley.'

He nodded understandingly. 'Of course, sir. Shall I leave the coffee in here?'

'Yes, Bradley; perfect. I think that's all for now, I'll see you downstairs in a quarter of an hour. Keep our guest entertained, will you... offer him some breakfast or something.' Bradley paced out the room and I made my way to the guest bathroom.

After completing my toilet I gulped down the coffee Bradley had left and proceeded down the staircase to the drawing room. I found Brivopolis seated in an armchair, a cup and saucer on the table next to him, immersed in one of the latest journals from London. I coughed and he looked up, rising as he did so.

'Good morning, Captain! My apologies for calling so early, but Hewitt sent a man round late last night to tell me that our passage has been arranged for mid-morning, so I thought an early rise would be best.'

'So this is what you call a morning in Greece! In England we would call this the devil's hour. Hewitt can go and cast himself into the pits of damnation for all I care; no human being deserves to have to rise at this ungodly hour. Cheroot?' I proffered the case I had withdrawn from my pocket.

'No thank you, Captain.'

'Suit yourself,' I said, striking up a match and watching the comforting glow of the tobacco spread through the whole cigar.

Brivopolis surveyed my little ritual and then continued. 'Have you all your things in order? Hewitt sent round a couple of carts. I have taken the liberty of taking one for myself and allocating the other to you.' I gave a curt nod and called for Bradley, who appeared swiftly.

'Bradley, oversee the loading of our cart, would you? I'll be out shortly. You wouldn't happen to know if the cook has prepared any breakfast, as I'm sure our guest is hungry?'

Bradley nodded and bustled off to see to my orders.

While the majority of household busied themselves in loading up the cart, a male servant brought breakfast to Brivopolis and me in the drawing room. We consumed our meal in silence, both of us being tired and having little inclination to engage in conversation. It did not take long for the servants to finish loading up Bradley's and my possessions and supplies, and so the cart set off. Brivopolis and I agreed to take some tea before making our way in a leisurely fashion to the docks, enjoying a final look at Venice and breathing in the rich heritage of the place for one last time.

The quays were already pulsating with activity by the time we arrived. Dawn was just breaking, but the darkness had been of no issue to the dock hands; work would often continue throughout the night with no break before the coming day. As the bleak light steadily revealed more and more of the grimy scene before us, we were exposed to the less romantic side of Venice. The docks were not home to ornate palazzos or grand piazzas, but rather to a collection of grim huts and a grubby smog and stench that hung over the area as a reeking cloud of industry. Gone were the richly decorated barges of the Italian and Venetian nobility, and in their place were the steamers and outdated Turkish galleons or *kalyonlar* that had been popular both among Ottoman admirals and civilians about thirty years ago, but were virtually obsolete against the warships of today.

We managed to pick out our carts, which had come to a halt beside a scruffy looking vessel, a Venetian galley by the look of things, and strode down to meet the servants who were busily unloading the household's possessions. I wasn't bothering to travel with a full accompaniment, only a cook and couple of servants, not including Bradley. Brivopolis was travelling much in a similar sort of fashion; we were hardly planning on setting up permanent camp in Constantinople.

We reached the little entourage and discovered much to my satisfaction that Hewitt had had to heave himself out of his bed and come down to oversee the loading of the ship, something Brivopolis had ensured. His thin and reedy voice seemed to squeal above the clamour that had infested the entire dock, dictating orders to the men that were everywhere, loading and unloading, making the ship seaworthy and ready for our expedition into the East.

I won't tire you with an account of this tedious part of my travels. Departure is never an exciting event, and this case was typical in the whole unremarkable nature of the affair. After a long period of hanging around, accompanied by a couple of cheroots, eventually the time came for us to depart. By now my excitement and enthusiasm for the adventure had considerably decreased (not a hard achievement, I assure you; I am rarely enthused before dawn, least of all when it concerns long and irksome journeys by sea). The captain was a ratty little Venetian with skin like an especially wrinkly walnut, a complexion like dark tea, and scent that would knock a Russian out. He approached and launched into some babble in Italian dialect, emphasising everything with ridiculously flamboyant hand gestures, giving him the resemblance of a dervish on opium. We watched this spectacle, a bemused expression creeping over both our faces, and met his exclamations with blank glances. Finally he paused, gasped a quick breath, then pursued another line of inquiry and, obviously deciding that his previous gestures had not been enough to convey his point, he proceeded to elaborate, contriving even more (if possible) spectacular movements to accompany the spew of Italian he was projecting onto us. Although I had studied Italian at university, the linguistic tangle that emerged from the captain's mouth did not bear any resemblance to the formal version of the language that I had learnt.

Eventually he came to a halt and began to look rather helpless, casting his gaze around him, searching for an interpreter. He caught Hewitt in his sight and dragged him over, much to his confusion. He then turned his fearsome speech onto the Englishman, making several jerks and glances in our direction until Hewitt began to nod sagely, muttering consent.

Hewitt turned to us. 'The captain says hello, and wishes you a pleasant voyage.' And with that he turned and then trotted off to see to some other menial task without another word.

The captain remained, beaming at us with a row of tobacco-stained teeth, seemingly mightily pleased with himself. I looked him up and down, gave a snort of derision and made off up the gangplank onto the ship, which was nearing the end of its preparation. Brivopolis accompanied me and together we weaved our way through the clutter and general flotsam and jetsam that crowded the deck until we came to the poop deck. We chatted idly for a while as the remainder of the preparations were carried out and before long the last cask was loaded on and the last rope secured tightly in its place.

Hewitt heaved his bulk up the gangplank and up to join us. 'It seems the time has come for us to say farewell. The pleasure in this meeting was great; indeed, it pains my heart to see you go, as it does at the thought of having to return to my lonely vigil in this perilous city. Hopefully you will not meet the same ghastly fate as Mr Burnes did, poor man. Either way, fare ye well, my friends, and tread carefully! The land of the Ottomans is a dangerous place at best, no land for God-fearing Christians like you and me!'

'Quite,' I said. 'Of course you are right, Mr Hewitt. If it was not for brave men like you and Mr Burnes, the empire would be a very different place. I for one will feel much safer knowing that I have my back covered by you, sir.'

Brivopolis gave me a sharp glance, obviously intended to keep me in check, lest the idiot realise the mockery I had been putting him through these last few days.

'Why, thank you, Captain. It is good to know that one's efforts do not go unnoticed.'

Brivopolis was to have his turn, and gave the man a brusque nod. 'Goodbye, Mr Hewitt. My prayers will go with you. Your services have been invaluable in helping us with our mission.'

Hewitt garbled out some rubbish about 'it was only the best that he felt he could offer', and how he was 'the humble servant' of both of us. Of course it was all sycophantic burble, and after his departing speech he wasted no time in making himself scarce and darting off back to the safety of his palazzo.

I turned to Brivopolis who was gazing at the docks, a pensive glaze over his eyes. I started him out of his reverie by saying, 'Well, at least we've cut loose the baggage from our coat-tails. Rather heavy baggage, I must say.' This provoked a smile out of Brivopolis. I continued, 'I suppose it's now that the real adventure begins. This entire business with Burnes is little more than a preamble to the real action. This whole thing goes far deeper than a simple murder, a fact Hewitt, I think, has failed to grasp. The one thing that worries me, though, is the involvement of the bloody Ottomans. Of all the devils we had to get involved in it had to be the accursed Turks. As my father said, "If he wears a towel on his head, he can't be trusted!" '

Brivopolis gave me a bemused look. 'I never quite understood the British sense of superiority. For a country that is so bizarre, so divided, so uniquely odd, I never understood what was meant to be so superior to other cultures!' He barked out a short, humourless laugh, and continued, 'Somehow we Greeks are supposed to view cricket as more sophisticated than several thousand years of democracy. Utterly bizarre!'

I replied with a haughty and what I thought was hopefully a superior and very British silence, and turned my attention to the ropes being cast away from the ship, and the lurching that had seized the vessel as we finally began to make our way out to sea. Brivopolis had retreated back into his thoughts once again, leaving me to ponder on matters by myself.

The journey was anything but the adventure I had been hoping for. The novelty (if there had even been one) wore off within days and soon I settled into the routine boredom experienced by so many sailors. Brivopolis said little, and I'd be damned if I was going to have a conversation with the captain, so I wrapped myself in books, chess and smoke, occasionally venturing out on deck to take the air; but on the whole I stuck to the rather fishy-smelling domain of my cabin. The weather remained mostly fair, although there were a few nights which, to use the expression most awfully, rocked the boat. Little occurred for those days, life becoming conformed into a dull and repetitive routine which held neither excitement nor pleasure, and which only succeeded in increasing my irritable mood. To make things worse, the captain kept a dry ship, something which hardly endeared him to me or the men, and resulting in me coming into possession of a truly filthy temper.

Our voyage had little of interest, and we took the usual route that the Venetians use on their trips to the city. After leaving Venice we sailed south, down the Adriatic, and, heading for the Greek coast, stopped off at Ragusa. We only berthed there for a day, but that was time enough to be able to enjoy the city. The old town and its magnificent walls were sights well worth a glance, which I got many as my companions and I wove our way through the tight-knit alleys until we burst out onto the town's main thoroughfare, a Romanesque boulevard that ran from the docks down to the town's famed cistern. While the crew took on supplies, Brivopolis and I, closely followed by Bradley, pottered through the city, enjoying the sunshine, blue skies and the general ambience of the place. After a while we settled down in a small inn and sampled some of the regional delicacies, mostly stuff of an Italian and marine influence – pasta and lobster and such like. Needless to say some of the region's liquid delicacies were also sampled, resulting in the return journey back through the port's winding alleys being rather trickier than the inward journey.

We promptly set sail after our return and headed south, to resume our journey around Greece. There wasn't really much to report for this leg of the journey. Most days I joined Brivopolis on deck as he pointed out Corfu, where we berthed briefly, and the more prominent of the Ionian Islands. Needless to say, I did not fare well on the boat. I could have paid a servant to slide my bed around my room and punch me in the stomach, which would have resulted in an altogether more pleasant effect than that constant swaying and rocking that I came to despise. Although we did not land on any of the islands, once we were on the eastern coast of Greece we made a night and a day's halt near Athens, berthing at some grubby little port.[5]

We passengers used this as a chance to visit the cradle of democracy, and so transport was arranged to the city. After an extremely uncomfortable journey we arrived in what could only be described as the world's only neoclassical hovel. Crowned by the Acropolis, what lay beneath was a combination of squalid huts and ruins and a vast building site, part of Otto's attempt to reinvent Athens as a great Western city.[6] Brivopolis was delighted to be able to return to his homeland, and shortly disappeared off into the city, obviously with his own agenda, no doubt to report to his superiors on the details of his mission so far.

With Bradley in tow we surmounted the summit of the Parthenon and proceeded to lap up the centuries of philosophy and innovation that had stemmed from the site. The scars the Turks and British had left were obviously visible, the former desecrating the site, turning it into a mosque and fortress, and the latter stealing whatever it could get its hand on to cart back home, as Elgin had so marvellously demonstrated. After a hard day of sightseeing and walking, Bradley and I settled for finding a tavern and refreshing ourselves sufficiently. And so it was that rather unsteadily we found our way back to the collection point, and after waiting some considerable time for our Greek acquaintance, set off on the return journey to the ship.

Sometime later he appeared with dusk on his heels, claiming he had finished his business and that we were to continue. I asked him to provide details of his adventure but he politely fended off my probing, and so we set off once more just before night fell properly, confined to that miserable floating hole that I had come

---

[5] The place that Simms scathingly refers to is Piraeus, the principal port of Attica and Athens.

[6] Hundreds of years of attacks, neglect, razing and sacking had left Athens (with the exception of the Acropolis) an almost temporary village of barely 5,000 inhabitants. Once invited to become king, Otto was charmed by the city's legendary reputation, and embarked on a vast reconstruction programme to make it a capital worthy of the town's history.

to loathe, and thoroughly confused and irritated by Brivopolis for being such a mysterious spoilsport.

It was later that night that we discovered that we were not to have a peaceful journey to our destination – indeed far from it. We had settled into our cabins for the night and I was relaxing and taking a rest, enjoying a cheroot and a book – James Buckingham's *Travels in Assyria, Media and Persia* (a most interesting commentary on those exotic and mysterious patches of the globe) – when I heard outside a clatter, like that of glass breaking, and a short fizz and footsteps hurrying away, followed by a splash. This odd pattern of sounds hardly seemed to be normal, so I sprang up casting my book aside and, clenching my cheroot firmly between my teeth, I advanced to the door.

Just as I opened it, I was driven back as a whoosh of flame swept up from the deck and mushroomed up, a wall of dry heat blossoming towards me. Gasping in shock, I staggered back. It was obvious that I would have to escape to my cabin, but the only door was hardly an option. Luckily by now the hands on deck had seen the predicament blighting their vessel and were rushing towards it to try and tame the blaze. It was, however, to no avail; their piteous attempts to quell the flames with the water butt in the centre of the deck failed miserably, and I continued to be trapped by the wall of fire that was slowly consuming my doorway.[7] I threw glances all around myself, desperately searching for something that would allow me to buy time or an exit from the furnace that my cabin had transformed into.

Suddenly it came to me! If I could make it, perhaps I could swing out of my window and down a deck into the cabin below! Grabbing my possessions that were nearest the flames, I piled them on the cabin bed against the far wall, placed my cheroot in the ashtray on my small table and heaved myself onto the window ledge. Beneath me the salty waters seethed and plunged in the dark, and just below I could make out a patch of light from the cabin. Above me there was a ledge and then the railing of the poop deck. Somehow it made more sense at the time to go up, the path downwards seeming just a mite too adventurous.

---

[7] It seems from his account that Simms' cabin in situated on the deck, rather than below deck, where the majority of passenger and crew cabins would be situated.

Grasping the ledge above firmly, I stood up in the window and after a few deep breaths leapt upwards, pulling my unwilling body up after me. I made a mad snatch for the railing, catching it with my right hand and dragged my torso onto the ledge and scrabbling with the legs hung over the void beneath, hanging over the boiling waters. My legs slipped over the side of the ship, grappling for purchase on the rough wood. Finally, after what seemed like an eternity, my left boot caught a protruding nail and, seizing my chance, I powered upwards with all my strength propelling my whole body onto the ledge and over the railing, where I slumped onto the deck, unnoticed by the hands.

The blaze now lit up the whole ship, seemingly originating from the deck itself, while the crew danced around, lobbing cold seawater onto it and babbling in panicky voices. Of the captain and Brivopolis I caught no sight, but Bradley had appeared by now and was organising the attempt to curtail the blaze. There was something wholly unnatural about these flames, and their refusal to be quenched. As I lay huddled on the poop, I sifted through the shelves of my mind, searching for an answer to our predicament. Suddenly it came to me! How could I have been so foolish? This was Greek fire!

I leapt to my feet, rejuvenated by my discovery, and charged down the stairs calling to the crew, 'Sand! We must throw sand upon it!' I seized a surprised crewmember and bellowed my instructions at him again, and off he scuttled in search of some sand. He returned with a sack of the stuff, dragging it up the steps behind him. I gestured for more of the crew to gather the sand and soon Bradley and I were herding them below decks while they emptied the sack's contents over the blaze, depriving the flames of oxygen.

Soon, as more sand was brought up, the fire began to die down, starved of its catalyst, until all that was left was a pile of hissing sand scattered over the deck and a black, charred hole where my cabin door had been. The crew gathered round the portal, murmuring in hushed voices, and I pushed myself to the forefront of their huddle and peered into the gloom. I caught a glimpse of something glowing in the darkness: my cheroot! Still lit, it had smouldered on unawares throughout the whole kerfuffle. A thought struck me, and I decided to indulge myself with some mild play-acting, for what better chance to play the hero of the hour?

Striding forwardly nonchalantly, I entered the cabin and made a beeline for the smoking cigar. Then, clamping it firmly between my teeth, I turned and addressed the crowd. 'And now that I've got your attention, what does one have to do to get a drink on this tub?' I could see a grin parting Bradley's lips, and was about to continue when the captain bustled onto the scene with Brivopolis in tow.

Immediately the man let loose a stream of his unintelligible dialect, furiously interrogating the nearest crewmember. Catching sight of me, he launched himself upon me, berating me with a tirade of incomprehensible protests and inquiries. When he paused to catch breath (for he was turning quite blue), I thanked him for his concern and took my leave, striding off to join Brivopolis on the far side of the deck, where he had taken in the whole scene with an amused expression playing on his lips.

'That was a pretty little show you put on over there,' he began. 'Quite the gentleman hero!'

I grinned at him, and drew deeply on my cheroot, sucking in the smoke, and turned to gaze out to sea, resting my other elbow on the balustrade. 'Well, it always goes down well to put on a bit of a show. Got to let them know we won't be intimidated by these sorts of antics!'

'You think the perpetrator is still on board?' Brivopolis exclaimed, a look of surprise on his face.

'Of course! Why, you don't think they would be able to flee out here, would you?'

'It seems so,' said the priest, gesturing to a cluster of the crew. 'They have discovered one of the ship's boats to be missing.'

As he said this, the captain joined us and began to bellow his despair and annoyance at this new misfortune that had befallen his vessel, smacking the watchman around the head for his carelessness.

I snorted with derision, muttering, 'Italians!' Brivopolis declined to comment on the subject. I suddenly realised that dawn was breaking, unfurling from the East, spreading a weak grey light across the whole tableau. There was obviously no chance of returning to my cabin or sleeping after the excitement of the night, and I was in no real mood to continue conversation, so I took my leave of Brivopolis and retired to the poop deck, to look out over the sea and lose myself in my own thoughts and a cloud of smoke.

We continued our journey across the Aegean with little issue. Some material was placed across the hole in my cabin wall, rendering it usable again, and I took up lodging there once again. After quite some while, we eventually approached the Dardanelles and changed course to make our way up the straights past the Gallipoli peninsula. When we reached this stretch we were confronted with the mighty forts which guarded the entrance to the straits, which I eyed cautiously. Brivopolis comforted me, though, telling me that it had been many years since the fortresses had been fully manned, and if rumour was true, since the huge cannons mounted on their walls had actually fired, or had sufficient powder to be armed. Indeed, on closer inspection the walls did appear to be crumbling, and the men upon them few, and many of the forts had the obvious signs of decay if one looked for them. Either way, we passed along through the Sea of Marmara unchallenged, watching the cliffs and rolling farmlands on either side float by, and hailing greetings to other merchant-men as they drifted past, laden with goods bound for Venice and Genoa.

After what seemed an exceedingly dull (not to mention dry) eternity, our voyage began to wind down and draw near to its end. I have to say that I almost skipped across the deck when I heard this news, and ordered Bradley to make our things ready for departure; I was not planning on spending any more time on our godforsaken tub than strictly necessary. The end was in sight, and it was not long till we caught our first glimpse of Constantinople, jewel of the Sultan's crown, a huge, heaving, pulsating mass of bodies, riddled with plotting, mystery and the exotic scent of the East; city of emperors, once the bastion of Christendom, and now a citadel of Islam.

Of all the cities that I had ever listened to tales about, Constantinople was always the greatest. Not even Rome came close to rivalling its magnificence, its size, its sights, smells or people. No other city on earth has the same unique blend, a huge melting pot of East and West, Mussulmen and Christians, all thrown together, each with their own unique tale to tell of that thriving metropolis. No other city has had quite such a rich tapestry of tales surrounding it; the great battles of Constantine, the fall of the West and the rise of the East, the golden years of Justinian, the adventures of the crusaders, the fall of the Byzantine Empire, and finally the twilight years of that giant of a city, a wounded colossus defending all Christendom from the darkness that would eventually smash through the gates of Constantinople and end at the gates of Vienna,[8] leaving whole kingdoms ravaged by war and whole cultures eradicated and changed for ever. The history of Rome seemed tame in comparison. And so we drew near to that city – city of emperors, mullahs, crusaders and sultans alike.

---

[8] The Siege of Vienna (1529), the first attempt by the Turks to capture that historic city. Led at first by Suleiman the Magnificent, they were eventually beaten back by John III of Poland in 1683 after over one hundred years of on and off sieges, meaning that Europe was released from fear of the Ottomans for the first time since the Battle of Mohacs.

Part Two
Constantinople

Chapter Five

A dull smog clutched the city in its grasp, hugging the low skyline as if determined to shroud the entire land in cloud. The proud dome of Haghia Sophia towered above the rest of the city, even more glorious with the addition of the Turkish minarets that tapered up to the sky at each of the church's four corners. The rest of the city slumped down to the waterfront, the dirty fug above disguising for the most part the grimy and low-lying sprawl that made up the bulk of the city, an eternity of winding passages and alleys, bustling bazaars and exotic harems. My eyes drifted down to the port, which was crowded with masts, all bobbing in the swell of the Bosphorus, and as we drew closer I was able to make out the hubbub of activity there – men swarming over the moorings and ships, laden with all manner of things, from spices to jewelled caskets, all evidence of the exotic riches the East held. Finally we had arrived, gulls wheeling over us, crying out a greeting, and a hubbub of noise swelling up across the water towards us.

Before long we were immersed in the scum and debris that lay on top of the water by the docks, and we were within throwing distance of the quayside. The captain piloted our vessel up to an empty berth and the mooring lines were thrown ashore. The crew proceeded to make the ship ready to land, and Bradley appeared above deck, informing me that we were ready to proceed. After a short while the buzz of activity on the ship slowed down and a gangplank was thrown down. Brivopolis led the way and Bradley and I followed. Brivopolis and I took a seat on the low wall that rimmed the harbour, and Bradley was left to oversee the unloading of our possessions. There was silence between us for several minutes as I took in the vast creature that was Constantinople. Hundreds of sights, sounds and smells overwhelmed my senses, and I was left speechless, only able to sit and absorb what I was faced with.

After a while, when I had tuned myself into the city, I absent-mindedly fished around in a pocket for a cheroot, and, striking a match off the rough wall under me, I lit up, puffing up a great plume of smoke which was twisted and brushed away by the mild and refreshing sea breeze. 'I suppose we'd better find somewhere to bunk down for the next few days,' I began. 'Shall we?'

Brivopolis and I rose and left Bradley to handle the menial business. We made for a grimy passageway that wound down the port, through a gaping hole into the reek of the city. We entered, and suddenly we were in an almost subterranean environment, houses crowding over the top of the alley, blocking out the sun, shrouding the whole scene in twilight. The noise of the port was muffled and distant, and a putrid smell – the smell of thousands of bodies cramped together, a smell of spice, smoke and sweat – surged towards us, enveloping us in its stink, something that my nasal passages still twinge at the thought of. It took a moment for our eyes to adjust to the gloom but we were soon able to pick out the people, the women and children that were huddled in the shadows, a low murmuring coming from the shades, ignorant of our presence.

As we made our way along the winding trail, we were further immersed in the heart of the city. The street wove itself steadily uphill, and as we progressed we were joined by more of the city's inhabitants. The way broadened, but rickety stalls hemmed us back in. All around us there was a vivid tableau of Ottoman life: old men clustered round tables, sipping sweet coffee, drawing on their pipes, hunched over the dice that clattered from their hands, turbaned men bustling past around us, children (no doubt thieves or some other form of vagabond) picked their way through the throng, spying out fresh victims and all the while the gulls wheeled above us, reminding us of the nearby sea. We were sucked into the throng, people of all sorts brushing past us, and the vast current of citizens propelled us up and along the street. We were helpless in trying to dictate at what speed we travelled or where we went; we merely floated up and up to the pinnacle of the city, the Haghia Sophia.

After what seemed an eternity we were finally spat out of the tunnels and found ourselves in a wide boulevard, the sun pounding down upon us, forcing us to blink after the dullness of the passages. We had arrived at the crown of Istanbul, Haghia Sophia, or to use its Turkish title, the Aya Sofya. Originally the testament of Justinian, the 'Church of Holy Wisdom' dated from the year 537, an astonishing feat of the Byzantine Empire. For over 1,200 years she had watched over her city, witnessing all of its chequered past. Empires had literally crumbled around her, but she had passed through it all. Now she called the Mussulmen to prayer from her four great minarets, issuing their ethereal wails across the city.

We paused for a moment to take in the sheer raw magnificence of what stood before us. Towering over all around us, the building's edifice frowned disapprovingly down upon at us, strangers spellbound by the marvel's majesty. However, we were not alone; indeed, I realised we had already drifted towards the doors, pushed by the tumultuous crowd. The brief freedom we had felt at being back in the sunshine swiftly disappeared as we were enveloped in a cavalcade of smell and noise, blanketed particularly in the raw odour of human bodies, which, when mixed with the rather more interesting smells of an eastern city and the blistering, constant heat, creates an almighty reek that permeates everything.

Brivopolis called over the din, 'Simms! Simms, my friend! Shall we head for the cathedral? Perhaps there we can find peace in the cool shade.'

I bellowed my consent back, and so we began to wrestle and scrummage our way towards the gigantic doors, pushing our way through the throng. It seemed an age before we were finally spat out into the narrow corridors of space that flanked the main thoroughfare and were mainly devoid of people. We had come out down to the right of the door, so we made our way up till we were eventually in front of the massive portal. We walked up towards it, skirting an elaborate ruin to our left.[9] Brivopolis approached the door, pushing open the carved wood, which swung open with surprising ease. A gust of cool air blew out, soothing our burning skin. We both sighed for a moment,

---

[9] This Byzantine frieze pictures sheep. Part of the original monumental entrance to the earlier church, the frieze has been preserved to this day.

Brivopolis leaning against the doorframe, sweat trickling down his face to be lost in the thicket of his greying beard.

I gestured, 'Shall we?' and allowed the priest to lead the way in. I followed him and was caught out by how dark it was in the antechamber. It was cool here, and for a while we both stood in the dark, silent. After a while Brivopolis began to explain the room we were in. 'This chamber is known as the outer narthex. And through there –' he pointed into the gloom – 'is the inner narthex.' He paused. 'How are you? I feel greatly refreshed now. Shall we continue?'

I nodded, and again he led the way into the inner chamber. As we entered he spoke again. 'And this, my friend, is the Imperial Gate.' He stopped, allowing the atmosphere and sight in front of me to sink in. Ahead of us stood a vast wall and gate, glowing gold and azure in the flicker of candles around us. The scent of incense wafted through from the nave to us, and the heat began to build again, enhanced by the thousands of candles clustered around us. Mullahs and laymen lurked in corners, whispering their concerns, adding to the mysticism and wonder of the place, snippets of foreign tongues drifting over to us on the smoke of the candles.

We left our shoes in the piles heaped against the walls and advanced towards the gate. We passed through unchallenged and emerged into the nave, that vast and domed space that occupied the centre of the building. In front of us was a huge towering opening rimmed by countless columns that stretched up and up until our straining eyes could pick out the golden seraphim that adorned the base of the bulging dome, a mighty crown nestled on a many layered stack of pillars, a gargantuan and awesome tribute to the architectural skills of the Byzantines and their successors, the Ottomans.

Brivopolis proceeded to point out to me the more historic of the mosque's features. Our gaze passed over the coronation square, where dozens of emperors had knelt and received the imperial crown, the Imam's *kursu*,[10] the Sultan's lodge and muezzin *mahfili*.[11] We decided to ascend to a higher level and

---

[10] *Kursus* only feature in some mosques. A *kursu* is the throne an imam will use when reading passages from the Koran.
[11] A large platform found in some mosques. The muezzin (mosque official) will stand here and chant responses to the imam's prayers.

thus survey the impressive hall in which we now stood. After a brief climb we found ourselves in the galleries that women used during prayer times. We approached the balcony and together viewed the pale floor that was laid out beneath us. People below scurried across the open hall or clustered in groups around the pillars, exchanging words in a low and dull murmur that floated up to us. We were alone in our position. Indeed, we were standing at the same height as the calligraphic roundels that clung to the pillars around the place. The Byzantines had designed the church to be a reflection of heaven, a celestial mirror, and in that aspect they had certainly been successful, for the whole place had a kind of ethereal feel, giving me the impression that what was in front of me wasn't quite real, rather a sort of dreamworld of gold and murmuring. I was lost in the magic of this amazing place and found myself picturing scenes from my schooldays, the emperors kneeling beneath the mighty dome, the erection of the tokens of Islam, the great Ottoman monarchs attentively listening to the wailing calls of the mullahs from their grand pavilion. I remained in this state for a considerate period of time, replaying the history of the mosque in my mind, trailing through the great tapestry that had been weaved around this one building.

Suddenly, out of the corner of my eye I caught a movement. I spun round, calling to Brivopolis as I did so, only to discover the priest was nowhere to be found. There was an uneasy silence and I cautiously advanced towards the stairwell from where I had heard the sound. I slipped my hand up into my jacket and found the polished butt of my pistol, which I gripped reassuringly. I stepped closer and closer and stopped just short of the opening. I braced myself and slowly willed myself to take the next step. I could feel my heartbeat quicken and stood stock-still, despite the beads of perspiration that were trickling down across my forehead and dripping onto my naked eyes, stinging with the salt. I blinked and swallowed, and suddenly I was very conscious of myself. How loud my heart sounded! The blood was pounding in my ears, and the sound of my breathing seemed like a gale in the still and heavy air of the mosque. Then, with all the will I could muster, I slowly lifted my foot up and let it hover for a moment above the stone flags.

'Simms!' Brivopolis' voice burst out behind me. 'Simms, what are you doing, my friend?'

I exhaled, relieved, and, slackening the grip on my pistol, turned to face the Greek. 'Brivopolis! What happened to you? I've been looking for you!' I examined him, awaiting a reply. Something was wrong, though. I felt something move behind me, and watched as the expression on Brivopolis' face turned from relief and complacency to panic and shock. Confused, I slowly turned to see in my horror shapes emerging from the very stairwell I had been about to examine minutes previously.

They sprang out of the shadows, one of them catching me off balance, knocking me to the ground with his shoulder. Despite the heat, they had wrapped thick scarves around their face and heads, much like the Bedouins of the desert. To my surprise they rushed straight past me, instead setting a course for the priest. Before I could react they had seized him, swiftly rendering him unconscious with a blow from a cosh one of them had concealed in their robes. Then, as if he were a child, one of their party swung Brivopolis onto his back and began to bear him away towards the nearest exit. However, they were not going to get away that easily. I began to rummage in my jacket, fighting to free my pistol from the trappings of its holster. I wrested it from its harness and pointing it in the direction of our assailants, I let loose a challenging cry.

For what seemed like the first time, our attackers took notice of me. One of them stopped, and retorted with something similar, only in his vile heathen tongue. I cocked my weapon, taking aim at his heart only to feel something looming above me. I looked up with trepidation to find my wavering gaze met by the cruel stare of none other than my quarry from Venice. I can say one thing for him: the bastard was an ugly fellow, and he leered delightedly at me, showing an uneven set of tobacco-stained teeth. I caught a whiff of his rank odour as he reached, to my horror, for his own cosh. I cried out and sought to turn my pistol on him, attempting to scramble up from the floor.

My attempts were to no avail, though, as in one swift movement he bore down upon me with his weapon, rendering me dazed with a crushing blow to my skull. Somehow I managed to stagger up, my drunken appearance providing my adversary with great amusement. My head lolled as I desperately searched for my firearm, and all the while my enemy eyed me up, picking a spot on which to finish me off. He advanced, kicking me in the ribs as he did so, knocking me to the ground, and my last memory was of him bringing his arm down on the back of my head, hurtling me into the deep darkness of unconsciousness.

Chapter Six

I awoke to feel something rough and damp being dragged across my face. The cool sensation was pleasing, although the object itself was coarse and stank of sweat. I urged myself to force my eyes open and found that I lay where I had fallen, collapsed in an incapacitated heap upon the flags of the gallery. The object, I discovered, was none other than a damp piece of cloth, a wet rag, and attached to it was a hand. Logic dictated that there was an arm and hopefully a body attached to this hand, and so I forced myself to crane my neck up and have a look at my saviour.

I was confronted with the astonished face of an old Turkish woman, who instantly began to babble away at some awful pitch. My eyes picked out my pistol, lying scattered on the floor a few feet away. The woman's gaze followed mine, and at the sight of the weapon she let out an agonising shriek and took flight, whirling out of the gallery and down the stairwell. I let out a low groan, uttered a few choice obscenities, and attempted to sit up. Attempted was the key word in this, as it took me several attempts to raise myself up, each resulting in my collapse, until finally I was able to heave my body up into what could pass as a sitting position, but was more a sort of crumpled slouch.

It was only then that I thought to carry out an inspection of myself. To my not complete shock I found my torso was covered in bruises, my neck painful and my face and clothes caked in dry blood. The woman's flight did not seem quite so much of a surprise now, as I resembled some sort of white-skinned berserker, covered in my own blood, groaning and cursing in harsh guttural tones. I suppose it must have been quite a shock for the old girl.

I patted myself down, running my hands over my crumpled outfit, and reached for my pocket watch. My hands only found air where the timepiece should have hung. I inwardly cursed the thieving piece of scum who had carefully prised the watch from the chain. It had been a prized possession, a gift from the family upon my appointment as a lieutenant not so long ago. However, I had been left my wallet and my pair of pistols. I restored the loose weapon to its home under my jacket, and with a great degree of wincing and gasping, pushed myself to my unsteady feet. I stretched, cracking my back, and proceeded to tenderly unbutton the front of my shirt and examine my battered body. My ribcage was covered in a large and dark bruise and I winced when I touched it. Luckily I didn't think I had broken anything, although my head was throbbing, and on running my hand through my hair I discovered a swollen lump where I had been struck.

Rubbing the back of my neck I replayed events, and the memory of Brivopolis' kidnapping came flooding back to me. I examined the gallery, looking for some sign that might lead me to the prisoner or his captors. There was, unfortunately, nothing. I think it would be fair to say that at this point I was completely lost; I had no clues and no point to begin my pursuit from. I lingered there for some time, unsure of what to do. Eventually, and with a heavy heart, I decided I would return to Bradley and the lodging he had found, where I would rest a while. It was with a heavy heart that I left the scene of Brivopolis' abduction, but it was plain to see that I could do nothing. I staggered towards the exit from the gallery and slowly lowered myself down the steps.

After what seemed an agonising eternity I once again emerged into the great nave. Ignoring the spectacular sight in front of me I headed straight for the gate, anxious to leave the place now. Collecting my shoes I hobbled back out into the sunshine and the sweat of the city. I must have been unconscious for several hours, as it was now well into the afternoon, judging by the position of the sun. With a sigh I was confronted with the vast, merciless and buffeting crowd and, taking a deep breath, plunged myself wholeheartedly into the throng.

Chapter Seven

Having battled my way back along the major thoroughfares, the streets began to get quieter as I grew closer to the docks. I stumbled along, soaked in my own perspiration, the pain in my side failing to abate. It was after roughly an hour in this fashion that I arrived back at the dockside, alone and bloodied. Bradley's jaw dropped at the sight of me. Shocked by my ghastly appearance, he cried out for help, dropped what he was doing and made straight for me. I batted away his hands and ordered one of the crew to fetch me a wet towel. Bradley probed me thoroughly, demanding to know what had put me in such a state.

'All in good time, Bradley. But first I think I need a wash and a drink. Have you located an inn?'

The always effective manservant had performed this task, having found one a short hobble away. I declared that we would set off for this place and staggered off, only to have to halt, gasping my side in pain. Thus I was forced to accept the support of Bradley's arm, and so, like a decrepit old man, I was helped along to the tavern where we were to stay.

The innkeeper was a rotund and jovial fellow with some unpronounceable heathen name. At our bequest he brought a basin and towel, a choice of meats, cheese and bread and a bottle of port, and led us to a table out on the street. I collapsed into a chair and proceeded to clean the blood and dirt off my face while allowing Bradley to pour me a glass of the port. He set the bottle down on the table and I jubilantly tipped the glass's contents down my throat. Sure enough, after a few seconds I felt myself relax and tingle, enjoying the feeling of the liquor coursing through my veins. I continued in this fashion for several minutes, slouched in silence, nursing my drink. Before long the bottom of my glass came into focus, but the cloudy glass was swiftly covered by the generous splash of port that Bradley was quick to supply.

I gestured to him, saying, 'Help yourself, I think we could all use a drink. On me, Bradley, on me.' I surveyed the dull scarlet slosh of the drink that Bradley swirled around in his glass. Reaching into my jacket pocket, grazing my pistol butt, my hand went in search of my cigars. However, my grasping fingers only found a large and unsettling space where there should have been a cigar case.

I exclaimed, 'I say Bradley! Don't have a cheroot on you, by any chance? Mine seem to have been stolen by those damnable heathens. What didn't they take?' Bradley fished around inside his jacket before pulling out a spare box of my favourites. 'Bradley, you genie! Marvellous. I swear I would be lost without you there to keep me straight. Have some more port; tonight I am going to treat both of us to a spot of fun. I need something to take my mind off the day's events.'

'Sir, if you don't mind me asking, what happened today… when you were out with Mr Brivopolis? Is he all right?'

'Bradley, I wish that I could say Brivopolis is all right. I'm afraid I can't. Today, when we were at the mosque, he was seized and I was attacked. Brivopolis was kidnapped, carried off by the shifty chap from Venice – the one with the beard I mentioned to you. I'm at a loss as to where to begin looking for him. They knocked me unconscious with a cosh – the villains – and roughed me up a bit. What really raises my blood is that the barbarian had the cheek to lift my watch. My damn watch, Bradley! It was my father's, and his before that. And from the look of things he might have taken a fancy to my cigar case! The rogue! So here we are, Brivopolis gone, no lead, no clues whatsoever. I can't guess where to even begin. However, for now, as far as I'm concerned, we can begin searching in the morning, but I am currently sore, battered and bruised and could use several more stiff drinks. Istanbul has a reputation for its back alleys, and I plan on exploring some of its choicer establishments tonight, if you would care to accompany me.'

Bradley agreed, and after a few more glasses of the fast dwindling port we both came to the conclusion that it was a capital idea. Before long the bottle was bereft of liquid, and so we bellowed for another bottle to be brought to our table.

I think it's rather obvious what sort of a turn that night took.

After a couple of hours we were riotously drunk, and scattering the collection of bottles that had come to populate our table, we set off in search of what for want of a better word was a whore-house. We found a particularly seedy hole in some scummy back alley, but from what I had heard this one was better than most, catering to the taste of Turkish army officers on leave in the capital.

Needless to say we had some roaring good fun (I treated Bradley to an education which only the British Army fails to offer when they recruit), and afterwards trotted off back down to our lodgings. Amazingly we were able to return unscathed, although I did have one hand on a pistol butt just in case; but if anything had happened I would have probably blown off Bradley's many blurring heads, upon which my other hand was leaning for support.

We trundled into our rooms in a lovely, drunken haze and collapsed in the rough cots, mostly oblivious to the troubles of the day, despite the constant nagging at the back of my mind that we were missing someone. I mentioned this to Bradley, bellowing something about him knowing of us 'being a chap down'. However he replied that he knew nothing about this matter, and so I drifted off, happily contemplating the spinning, dirty, stained roof of our miserable lodgings.

Chapter Eight

I awoke the next morning to a pain which compares to no other. Being shot is not a patch on the anguish that is the morning after a heavy night's drinking. I contemplated getting up, but then the pounding thud of the headache whirled into action, pinning me to my bed and putting all thought of going anywhere out of my mind. Best to remain in bed, I thought. In the cot opposite, Bradley was going through similar motions, clutching his throbbing forehead with a sweaty palm and muttering to himself behind closed eyes. I forced myself to wrench open my eyes but shut them almost immediately, blinded by the fierce stream of morning sunlight that was pouring into the grotty hole we had picked to spend the night in.

Shielding my face this time, I took in the dank little place. I have to say I preferred it when it was spinning, that way I couldn't look at any of it for more than a second. I heaved myself up, braving the pain, and relieved myself in the fetid pot that my hand found under the bed. I would have to talk to Bradley about finding new quarters. I found myself wondering where Brivopolis had spent the night, probably somewhere slightly nicer than this hellhole, knowing the sly old dog...

Then it hit me: *we'd lost Brivopolis*. A quick backtrack through the muddled events of last night to that afternoon. The cathedral, the attack, the kidnapping... my watch! The heathen bastards!

'Bradley!' I groaned across the room, if you could call it that. 'Bradley, you lazy dog, wake up!' I staggered across, still dressed in my crumpled outfit from the previous day, and shook the dozing servant. 'Get up!'

Lurching back to my corner I stripped down to my underthings and, taking cold water from the jug on the dresser, splashed it over my face, before turning and doing the same to Bradley. This was not met with delight, but rather a gurgle of mumbled oaths, so I threw a bit more on him for good measure before kicking him for being an 'insolent whoreson'. Needless to say, this treatment soon got him up and preparing himself for the day to come.

Finding Brivopolis might require me to be rather more discreet about my inquiries than usual. The distinctive red jacket and white breeches would instantly mark me out from the horde of international travellers that would usually be found in such a metropolis.[12] I ordered Bradley to keep his civilian clothes on as well. I'd rather have Bradley as my servant and spy than a guard, hoping that I would not need to employ him in that capacity. Looking to check the time, out of pure habit, my hand swept up to my front, only to grasp thin air, reminding me of the thieving scum who had taken Brivopolis from us. Bradley, seeing my predicament, informed me that it was almost a quarter to eleven! I had hoped to be up and ready at nine. Bradley was ready by now, and we made our way downstairs to the bottom floor of the tavern for a spot of breakfast and to plan our next move. I had to admit I was completely at a loss as to where to start.

Bradley and I procured our table out on the street, and while waiting for the owner to bring us whatever fare he could rustle up I pondered over the dilemma at hand. I thought it best to keep this very much a private affair. No sense in involving the consulate in the city; the last thing this matter needed was two dozen redcoats blundering around and trampling any clues there were in the city underfoot. I needed to keep our opposition as in the dark as we were. If they twigged that we were on their trail then they would simply melt away into the chatter and hubbub of Constantinople. It would make sense to return to the scene of the crime, to see if there was anything that we could glean from the site, as I must profess I was so in shock and flustered when I regained consciousness there that I didn't really think to examine the surrounding area.

The proprietor appeared at my left shoulder bearing a tray

---

[12] It seems that rather than find more opulent apartments and use his batman more as a servant and a personal dresser (as many gentlemen officers of the time would have done), Simms prefers to treat Bradley more as a friend and travelling companion whose services he requires occasionally. Bradley seems to be more a manager of Simms' affairs than his servant. The uniform that Simms would normally put on would be that of the 'Buffs', the 3rd Kent regiment.

laden with bread, cheese and oil, as well as a carafe of water and a pot of Turkish coffee. I eagerly poured myself a cup of the steaming coffee but thought I would leave the water, having seen the fetid pool from where the citizens drew their own supply. The coffee itself was vile, being sweet and sickly, but it was hot and countered my pounding headache. Bradley and I then proceeded to tuck into the bread and cheese, leaving any conversation to be returned to after our meal. After a good few minutes of silence and chewing, I swallowed the last of the food and leant back, lighting a cheroot, exhaling the smoke in a great plume over my head and pondered over the options for the day. Yes, to return to the mosque would make sense, but would there really be any clues for us? There was nothing for it, no other lead was available to me, and so I resolved that Haghia Sophia was the way forward. Bradley was rubbing his eyes, still trying to throw off the doziness that hung over him. I outlined to him my plan, declaring that we would leave as soon as he had finished his meal and I my cigar.

Feeling greatly refreshed and ready to face the challenges of the day, I clattered to my feet and motioned to Bradley to toss a coin onto the table for the food. Then we were off, swept up again into the great stream of people, bustling from place to place. It wasn't too long before we were in front of the grand mosque, and after pulling ourselves free of the stream of bodies I entered the structure once again, this time heading straight to the upper galleries, dragging an amazed Bradley behind me. I rushed up the stairs in my eagerness, and burst out from the claustrophobic darkness into the cool space of the gallery, casting my eye around for any sort of sign.

It was as I feared; there was nothing. Not a trace of the encounter remained on the site. A thought struck me, however. The exit through which our assailants had dragged Brivopolis beckoned invitingly at the far side of the balcony. Perhaps in that shadowy doorway lay the answer to retrieving my Greek companion. Calling Bradley over, I approached the stairwell, peering down into the gloom. Tentatively I stepped into the darkness and strained my eyes in the murk, looking for some sort of clue. There! My eye caught something – a scrap of paper – wedged into a corner of one of the stairs. I dove for it, clamping it in my hand and unfurled it, wondering whether this could be the key to the Greek's capture. I fumbled with the note, pulling at it, hastily trying to undo it, trying to discover its secret, if it had any.

Rakeeb Il Muthal

Three words, scrawled across the parchment in rushed Greek lettering, in what was most definitely Brivopolis' angular, jagged hand. Three words, which had no significance to me whatsoever. Who was this Muthal? What bearing did he have on this whole affair? No matter how hard I stared at the characters they had no meaning for me. Slumping down on the step, I crumpled up the paper in my hand, stretched out my legs and became aware of Bradley hovering behind my shoulder.

'What do you make of this?'

I proffered the note to him without turning, and he reached down and took it from me. A few seconds of silence ensued, and I sat in the gloom listening to Bradley's breathing, waiting while the man pondered over the scrap of parchment.

Another dead end. Where had Brivopolis gone? Who had taken him? All these questions raced through my mind. This matter had gone far further than a personal level. Brivopolis was in possession of important government secrets, secrets that could be catastrophic for Britain and her war effort if the wrong people knew about them. Did Brivopolis have a clue that I didn't? Either way, I needed his help. Without those papers there would be no evidence of the proposed Turkish attack, no evidence or hint for how the commanders in the Crimea could possibly defend themselves against the Turkish menace. Yet there seemed to be no way forward. No lead beckoned to me; all paths seemed closed.

'Sir?'

Bradley's question roused me from my melancholy reverie.

'Yes, Bradley, what is it?'

'If I'm not mistaken, sir, I think I may be holding the lead that you were looking for.'

'What? You know this Rakeeb Il whatever? You know this man? Who he is?'

'I'm afraid I can't answer all of those questions; all I know is that Mr Brivopolis mentioned that this man was an informer of his, a contact that he had in the city, and he'd arranged to have a meeting with him this morning. I'm sorry it took so long to remember, it's just that he mentioned it in passing, when we disembarked.'

I could have hugged him! Finally, a light at the end of the tunnel that was this awful, twisted, dirty mess. A clear trail among the heaving, winding alleys of this great metropolis!

But wait... There was one piece of crucial information that Bradley had not provided. We could not search the whole city for this one man. Could I dare to hope that Bradley would have the answer to my next question?

'And do you know where we can find this man?'

A pause, a smile, and then, 'I believe I do, sir.'

Chapter Nine

The Grand Bazaar is possibly the only place on earth where one can claim to be able to buy absolutely anything. Name your item, name your price, and for the chink of a few coins into a stranger's hand, that thing can be yours. Nowhere compares to this place; nowhere else would you find such an eclectic mix of cultures, blended together like the herbs and spices used by the perfume merchants. The result was a vibrant melting pot – a magnificent tribute to the world of trade.

Above my head the low, vaulted ceiling compressed this world down to a tunnel-like warren, echoing to the bawling cries of the merchantmen at work, advertising their wares to all who would stop for but a second to examine some trifle on display. All around me was a blur of colour, a haze of scents and shifting myriads of people, wrapped up in this world of bartering and haggling. I slowly turned on the spot, greedily trying to eat up all that I could take in, entranced by everything I saw, overwhelmed by the exotic, amazing atmosphere that filled this breathtaking place. To my right a merchant shovelled spices from sacks onto a set of scales, making small talk to his waiting customer, while on my left an old man sat on a stool, hailing passers-by with an invitation to his stall, gesturing to the rows of leather sandals like the ones he held in his withered hands, carefully piercing one with a long and deadly looking needle, tugging the thread through, binding the parts together.

Beside me Bradley stood in silence, soaking up the ambience of the place, as impressed as I was, and so we remained for almost a minute, the only movement from us being the slow, bewitched blinking of our astonished eyes, the gradual rotation of our heads and the raising of a hand to bat off the occasional urchin-cum-pickpocket.

Eventually, I realised that we would have to move on; there was business to be done here. Tugging Bradley by the arm, I muttered for him to follow and I made for the nearest stall, targeting the old man with the sandals. He leapt up when he saw our interest in him, assuming it was his wares we were after. Dancing around us on his bowed legs, waving his products in our direction, it took quite some time and some stern words to calm the fellow down. After a while he realised that we were not interested in procuring some new footwear, and sat back down on his stool, confused, and put on a haughty air, eying us suspiciously. I approached him and, pulling out the note, showed it to him, and said the name out loud.

He snatched the scrap off me and peered at it with half-blind eyes and pondered over the letters for a few minutes. Suddenly he burst into a stream of gibberish, babbling away in their inane tongue at me as if I had offended him in a most awful way. Then he turned around and hobbled into the depths of his shop, a sort of cavern in the walls of the bazaar, wailing. He disappeared for several minutes, although Bradley and I continued to hear him screeching and moving around inside. Eventually he emerged, dragging a boy behind him, and pushed the scraggly creature towards us, presenting him with a flourish, grinning at us through his three blackened teeth.

Of course, we greeted this with utter bemusement, wondering why the man was choosing to thrust his boy upon us. Was he offering him as a batman? A guide for the city, perhaps? Our question was soon answered when he handed the note to the boy, gibbering excitedly. The boy nodded slowly, stepped out into the main concourse and pointed down the way before turning to us and gesturing for us to follow. Then he trotted off. I hurriedly thanked the old man, nodding to him, and set off behind his boy, while he bowed and gleefully rubbed his hands together.

Trying to keep up with the urchin was a battle in itself, for he was clearly a veteran of the bazaar, ducking and weaving his way through the throng, threading through tiny gaps between strangers chatting outside a stall while Bradley and I blustered and blundered on our way behind him, desperately trying to keep up. We continued in this hectic fashion for quite some time; indeed, Bradley almost knocked a man down. I'm glad he didn't, for he was a heavyset character, who glared at us behind a swarthy black beard with smouldering eyes.

Finally, the boy began to slow down ahead of us, and began to search for something, eagerly looking to his left and right, trying to find the lair of the illusive Rakeeb Il Muthal. While he paused, Bradley and I were able to catch up, coming to a breathless stop at his side. We had come right to the very depths of the huge construction, having battled our way from the fringes to the epicentre of the bazaar, where the air was heavy with the rich spices and perfumes that the traders had on offer, giving the whole place a drowsy quality. It was less busy here. Gone was the torrent of punters who inhabited the corridors close to the gates; this was where the real merchants plied their trade, and all around they huddled in small groups in the shadows of their shops, the air full of their murmuring as they discussed the finer points of their business and the affairs of the world at large.

The boy motioned towards a large opening ahead of us, festooned with lamps and lanterns of all shapes and sizes on the walls all around it. The whole shop had an ethereal feel to it, and unlike its neighbours it sat in shade, the darkness accentuated by the sheer concentration of wares on display. There were no windows out to the pale sky here, the only light being the enchanting, flickering glow of the dull, blood red lamps that adorned every inch of the dark blue tiles lining the man-made cavern.

I turned to ask the boy to inquire after the owner, only to find he had gone, disappeared off into the ebb and flow of the human tide that flowed through this rabbit warren, slipping away without either Bradley or myself noticing his departure.

Once again I pulled out my scrap of paper, and taking a last look at the scrawled name upon it, folded it up once more and shoved it back into my jacket pocket and advanced into the gloom.

As soon as I entered I was sucked into a strange otherworld, bathed in the scarlet light emanating from the hundreds of fairy lights around me. Looking down, it seemed as if I had been soaked in the blood of a dozen men, so red was the light from the countless lanterns around me when cast onto my jacket. There was no sign of anyone else, and I began to lose myself in the endless hall of lamps and mirrors, forgetting even the silent presence of Bradley at my side, equally entranced by the incredible charm of the place.

And so we remained for a pleasant while, drifting through this subterranean plane, oblivious to the lesser world outside, cut off in a bubble of perfect light and silence, our faces youthful and eager once again when illuminated in the rich and luxurious glow of hundreds of trembling flames.

Eventually Bradley gently nudged me, dragging me back from my blissful reverie. 'Sir, this Il Muthal chap...' His voice sounded harsh and crude, ripping through the peaceful silence of the place.

I replied with some annoyance, 'And what of him?'

'Well, are we not here to find him?'

'Yes. I suppose you're right, we must move on, find this fellow. What time is it?'

A pause, and I hear a rustling behind me as Bradley fumbles for the timepiece he keeps in his pocket. '*Oh!*'

'What is it, Bradley?'

'My watch, sir, gone! Ah... wait now; I thought I felt that boy brush past me as he left. Filthy Turk! Sir... could I perhaps have permission to return to that shop we left from, and perhaps confront the brat about the matter?'

I replied, 'Of course. And while I wait I shall investigate, see if there is any evidence of this character around.'

Bradley shuffled out and burst out into the space and light of the corridor, blinking a few times before hastening off in the direction we came from, and I was left by myself in the gloom.

Suddenly felling very, very alone, I looked around for any sign of another person in the cave. I thought to explore the recesses of the shop, making my way right to the very back, where the shadows congregated together in dark huddles, casting the ornate carpets on the walls behind them into shade, dull patterns hidden away from the light of the lanterns.

I gave a tentative call into the murk. 'Hello? Rakeeb Il Muthal?'

Silence.

I let out a long sigh; another dead end in this infernal puzzle. I could see no other part of the shop besides this one large room, leaving me at a loss as to where this man could be. I decided to get out myself, to go in search of Bradley and return at another time, when perhaps I could find the stall's proprietor. I started to make headway to the exit of the den.

I don't know what it was that induced me to stay for that extra few seconds, hovering by the mouth of the shop, but it changed the course of this whole affair, and little could I have guessed the implications of that moment of hesitation.

He was a wizened old man, ancient, but certainly not frail. This was not a man that you double-crossed. Like a gnarled old tree, he was tough, and you could see from his appearance he was an intelligent man, a politic man. He lurched out of the shadows, muttering to himself, clattering his way through his lanterns, oblivious to my presence, tending to his wares, relighting those lights which had died out with a long taper he clasped tightly in his right hand. It was an intriguing sight, watching the elderly Ottoman hobble from lamp to lamp, whispering to them like they were children, a family of light that hung, obedient and vulnerable all around him.

After a few seconds I felt that I should make my presence known, and so I rasped out a cough, cutting through his muttering like a steely blade, shattering the quiet whispers that floated through the air from the hunched figure.

He fell silent and straightened up, twisting and craning his neck upwards to peer at me from under his felt hat, and gave a glare such as I have never seen before, locking my eyes to his with a fierce gaze of utter contempt. Nevertheless I pressed on.

'Rakeeb Il Muthal?'

He continued his scrutiny for a few seconds before relinquishing his stare, giving a short sharp nod of his head, his fez bobbing up and down as he did so.

'Can you help me? I'm looking for a Greek priest...' It suddenly struck me that I had never discovered Brivopolis' first name. I trailed off, leaving the words hanging, waiting for his reaction.

'Brivopolis?' He croaked out the name, rasping it in a reedy, heavily accented way, making it almost unintelligible, but nonetheless the right name.

My heart began to pound. Could this be the clue I had been looking for?

'Do you know where he is? Have you seen him?' I asked excitedly, rushing the words.

A nod.

I could have danced! Of all the places, all the people, this bizarre (and blatantly mad) old man held the key to my friend's whereabouts. I had finally found the lead I had been so desperately searching for.

There was little time to celebrate, though, as the Turkish gentleman was already limping away back into the depths from which he came, gesturing with an ominous finger that I was to follow him.

It transpired that his lair was hidden behind the layer of carpets that coated the shop, as he heaved one of the heavy rugs to one side, revealing an ornately furnished room behind. It was lit up with the glow of several Arabian lamps, casting a bright orange light over the chamber. A large futon heaped with cushions occupied one side of the room, while on the floor, walls and roof were more of the richly decorated carpets I had seen concealing the entrance. In the centre of the room was a low table with a coffee set on it, and on the floor beside that a large hookah, which had obviously only been recently lit.

My host gestured for me to sit on the futon, while he busied himself over serving the coffee, and after a few moments he handed me a steaming cup of the sickly stuff. Still he said nothing, and so I politely waited for a short period before deciding that I would have to instigate this conversation.

'You mentioned that you saw the priest? Or that you knew where he is or could be? You wouldn't care to elaborate on this, would you?'

He was now hunched over the pipe, and batted away my inquiries with an upraised finger while he added tobacco into the contraption. After battling with the hookah for about a minute he abruptly seized a mouthpiece and thrust it in my direction, waiting for me to take the proffered pipe before squatting down on the floor and sipping his coffee.

I could hardly refuse the old man, and anyway, I had always

been intrigued by the bubbling pipes of the Ottomans, and so I raised the tasselled mouthpiece to my lips and sucked…

A blurry shape swayed in front of me, rocking back and forth, while around me was a gloomy chamber of shadows, barely lit. Terrifying scenes drifted in front of my eyes, and I felt weightless, as if I was floating in some horrific wraith world. Distant figures swam in and out of focus before me, while screams and cries, strange voices echoed up to me, reverberating around the empty cavern of my mind; and then darkness rose up from the creature ahead, devouring me in its shadow.

Chapter Ten

I was lying on cool stone flags, drenched in sweat, and I could taste something foul in my mouth. I ran my dry tongue over my cracked lips, unable to open my clenched eyelids; all the while my head pounded in the background, the blood pulsing to my mind beating out a painful rhythm.

I might as well have tried to move a mountain as tried to get up. My body felt as if it were made out of lead, and was held down by dozens of weights, pinning me down to the cold floor. I lay there for about a minute, not having the energy or the will to stir my painful body. Eventually I forced open my eyes, immediately closing them again, for even the gloomy light was searing in its brilliance. After several more attempts I was finally accustomed to the dim light, and was able to take in some of my surroundings. Once again I was in the grubby chamber that I briefly remembered from before. It was small, and seemed to be some sort of cellar or back room, as there were no furnishings and the walls were of bare stone. After taking in my surroundings for quite some time I ventured to try and move my arms. It was a huge effort, but after some considerable strain I managed to jerk my arm. To my great surprise I found out I was not the only person in the room. My movement had provoked reactions from the chamber's other occupants, who muttered in Turkish, and then came some gruff tones from a source I immediately recognised.

Brivopolis.

A dozen questions raced into my mind. Was he safe? Was he hurt? And then something began to strike me as odd. Why was he here? A pair of feet planted themselves in front of me, and a pair of hands hauled me roughly up, tossing me onto a chair which had been drawn up behind me. My head lolled as crude cords were yanked around my wrists and ankles, pinioning me to my sole means of support. A hand lifted my chin up and strained my neck up and up until I found myself gazing into a set of piercing grey eyes. A wider inspection revealed that they belonged to none other than my former accomplice. By this point I was completely at a loss as to what was going on. I was utterly confused. Why did Brivopolis not release me? Why was I tied up in the first place? As all these questions dashed through my head, only an exclamation of surprise and inquiry blurted out, prompting a chuckle from my friend.

'Oh, Simms, dear, naive Simms, what a fool you are, and what a simpleton you have taken me for. It was so obvious! All this time, before your very eyes, and you never guessed. Did you not think? The signs were all too clear. The Greek fire, my disappearance in Athens, your assailant in Venice, perhaps? And may I suggest for consideration my… *kidnapping*.'

He lingered on the word, mockingly, giving the impression that it was a horrid and bitter taste in his mouth of something unsavoury. When I actually thought of it, these things all seemed peculiar and highly dubious. Replaying Brivopolis' capture in the mosque for a second time, the kidnappers' movements seemed unusually forced, and Brivopolis had yielded to their attacks easily, almost allowing himself to be borne off. As for the episode of the Greek fire, although I hadn't paid it much attention at the time, Brivopolis had been the last up above deck, and had seemed unusually bitter in our conversation afterwards, and disinclined to talk. Even his uncharacteristic absence in Athens seemed to hide some cunning and evil motive now.

I was blown away, speechless. The betrayal burned, red raw and fresh. I only had one question left for him now, and was able to utter it with bitter ease this time.

'Why?'

'Ah, the question we've all been waiting for. Why? Why? Why is because of the answer to all these cases. Why is because of money. Golden, filthy, but brilliant money. With money one can buy anything in this world, power, status… women.' His face twisted into a lecherous grin, for I now realised, this man was no priest, nor of any faith.

'Yes, Simms, I am not Father Brivopolis, rather Nikolai Lyubomir, and I'm no Greek either, instead an Ottoman

Bulgarian from Edirne. It's taken many years to get this far, slowly working my way up in the ranks of the janissaries, until, with my knowledge of English, I was given this most important task, with orders from our generals to secure those papers that you so eagerly and desperately search for. This is the end, Simms. I have the papers now. That traitor, Quatal, was removed by my accomplices here, copies were sent to our generals long ago, and plans are in motion which will crush you and your French allies. The papers are hidden, in a location which only I know. We are all too aware of what you would do when this war is won, the same as you always do. The Ottoman Empire is no cripple of Europe yet, and the last thing we need is a British-ruled Crimea and a Sultanate offering homage to an Anglo-French overlord! Within the month the attack will have begun, and ships of your wounded will be weaving their way back to Portsmouth, more even than your beloved Nightingale can cure.'

He barked out that short, sharp laugh of his, which in light of recent events seemed mocking and bestial, like the call of a hyena, brandishing a scrap of paper in his hand, resembling the note he had left.

'I've tried to kill you, throw you off the scent – I was simply beside myself when you appeared here, searching for me, and instead finding Rakeeb – and I've tried to buy time to find the papers. After today, Ottoman intentions will be secure. You have failed in your mission, and there is no use for you here now. Finally I have you to myself, and I can remove you from this mess and begin to enjoy my new-found wealth. Captain Simms, I salute you.'

With that last word, Brivopolis – or Lyubomir, as he now was – threw an almighty punch, crushing my nose to a bloody pulp. Then he took a staff that leant against the wall and thrust it into my torso, cracking a rib in the process. I breathed heavily, gasping for air as blood poured in a torrent over my face. I slowly and painfully raised my head again, staring my persecutor in the eye, braced myself for the final blow which would almost certainly render me unconscious, if not dead. Brivopolis raised the staff over his head, and gloatingly muttered out his last few words, 'Farewell, Simms, you bloody-minded fool!'

I closed my eyes as I heard the staff come hurtling down, and then came a huge crack.

But the blow never came. Slowly I opened up my eyes, my face still tense and clinched, and I gradually peered around. At my feet lay the slumped body of the so-called priest. In the side of his head was a gaping hole.

At the entrance to the dingy chamber stood Bradley, faithful Bradley, and in his hand an upraised pistol, pointing down at the huddled corpse below me. I could have leapt for joy, apart from the rather obvious inhibition of being strapped to a chair.

'Bradley!' I said rather thickly, slurring my words through my bloodied nose. 'Wonderful to see you. Simply wonderful.'

He just stood there, looking inquisitively at the body.

'Oh, that! Yes, I'll explain that in a minute, if you wouldn't mind helping me out with my current predicament.'

After a couple of moments sawing with a pocketknife I was free, and my bonds slipped to the floor while I gingerly stepped over Brivopolis' motionless body. I stood, fascinated, gripped by the cadaver lying sprawled on the flags. Bradley finally turned away and busied himself with mopping the sweat off his forehead with a handkerchief. I knelt down to examine the body, and noticed something in the fake priest's outstretched hand. It was the note he had brandished so fiercely at me, clamped tightly in his dead fingers. I prised it out and was placing it in my pocket when Bradley turned.

'Shall we, sir? I can't say that I'm anxious to remain around here for much longer.'

'Quite right, Bradley. Shall we give him a pat down and then head off?'

Together we set about searching the body, and with a cry of delight I removed my prized silver cigar case, and after I had tenderly secured it in an inner pocket we continued our search. Finding nothing else interesting, we heaved Lyubomir's corpse into a corner and covered it up with one of the carpets from the next room. It turned out there was a hidden entrance leading to this chamber off the room in which I had been drugged. As we passed through, I took the chance to examine the infamous hookah. One glance within the dish revealed that my speculations were correct and that it was opium which had addled my mind sufficiently to render me incapable of both movement and speech.

However, I'd had enough of this place and, eager to escape from the den, Bradley and moved on, storming out into the dim shop of lanterns, of whose owner there was no sight. I had no time for his wares on this occasion; all I desired was to get out into the open air, away from the claustrophobic interior of the lair.

We burst out into the brightness of the concourse, and once again I shielded my eyes, so strong did the light seem in comparison to the shop. After waiting a few moments for my eyes to adjust, it transpired that this part of the bazaar was in reality palely lit, a weak light percolating down from the distant openings above. It was deathly still here, the working day was drawing to a close, and we could glimpse twilight descending on the city far above us.

I didn't pay much attention to our journey back. As I floated along through the emptying streets of the bazaar, exhausted, in a dream-like state, all I wanted to do was return to our lodgings and collapse into my cot. Bradley steered me home as a mother guides a wayward child, and after what seemed an eternity we were once again standing in front of the grubby inn where we had based ourselves, and night had enveloped the city. Without any further words we both ascended to our room and settled down for a well-earned night's rest, my brain too tired to even begin contemplating the startling revelations of the day.

Chapter Eleven

We slept late that morning, exhausted after the exertions of the previous day. My brain was still stumbling behind, trying to come to terms with the treachery of Brivopolis and his death. In the light of day it all seemed so clear, and an hour or so over a leisurely breakfast dispelled any doubts that I had had. I now no longer though of my former ally as a Greek priest, rather as Lyubomir, Bulgarian spy.

However, more important things were afoot, such as the issue of the plans. Now that the whole disastrous scale of the plot was revealed to me, it seemed that Bradley and I were helpless to do anything to prevent the annihilation of our armies in the Crimea. I was at a loss what to do. I had no clear information, only that the Ottomans had violent intentions towards the entente in Russia, which our commanders already knew. What were needed were precise commands, plans and troop movements to enable our men to counter the Turkish offensive, and these could only be found on Quatal's papers. But where we could find the elusive papers was a mystery.

Irritated, I leaned back in my chair and reached for a cigar, and upon fumbling for my case my fingers brushed a scrap of paper. I pulled it out with the case and examined it. It was the note which had been clenched in Lyubomir's fingers when he had died, and was entirely unremarkable save for a line of Greek lettering scrawled upon it. Dragging my mind back to my school days, I roughly translated the words as an address, outlining what must be Lyubomir's lodgings. Delighted, I leapt to my feet and eagerly informed Bradley of my discovery. When all was lost, we had been handed this golden opportunity to complete our mission.

Only one thing remained now: to head for Lyubomir's rooms in the city, and we set off at once. So great was our excitement that we forgot to finish or pay for our breakfast and sped off up the street, eager to reach our destination.

After bawling the name excitedly at several sets of rather alarmed looking old men, we were able to discern the rogue's dwelling place from their startled directions. As I had expected, it was a dingy hole of a place. I noted dryly that Lyubomir had obviously not been paid for his treachery yet, and was grimly satisfied. I had no time to dilly-dally and so, calling Bradley to my side, I ordered him to draw his pistol. I did likewise, and with a butt in each hand I barged through the door and found myself at the foot of a squalid stairwell. Stretching my weapons out in front of me, I progressed up the stairs slowly, keeping a lookout for anything that might have been amiss.

The coast was clear, and we ascended the flight without any trouble. At the top a woodworm-ridden door swung softly from its hinges, opening up onto a grubby and poorly lit apartment. I stormed in, but was momentarily deterred by the great stink that arose from the room. Obviously Lyubomir had not been famed for his cleanliness. The bed was a morass of filthy sheets, while papers and clothes lay in heaps on the floor. In the corner was a bureau in a similar state of disarray. The stumps of cheap candles were stuck to the poor quality wood, and streams of wax had dripped down onto some of the papers themselves. I made a beeline for the desk, kicking aside the fetid piles at my feet, and cast my gaze over the surface, searching for anything which might resemble an official document.

Nothing.

Dismayed, I continued to search, but it was in vain. My hunting was to no avail, the papers were nowhere to be seen. However, as I turned to face Bradley, something caught my eye, almost obscured by a molten flow of wax: a locked drawer.

But the key was not around. Wait! What a fool I was; here I was with a pair of pistols in my hands and I was looking for a key…

'Bradley, stand back, you might want to cover your ears.'

Taking careful aim, I let loose the ball, splintering the wood and shattering the cheap lock. The ball had rebounded, skittering into a corner, luckily not hitting either Bradley or myself. I heaved the drawer open and with delight found in my hands a sheaf of rich, thick and creamy paper. I slowly perused the pages, taking in the lines of bold and flowing Arabic script, which although incomprehensible, were quite obviously of an official nature. I stowed them away in a leather wallet on the desk, which I then gave to Bradley while I continued to rifle through the desk's drawers just in case there were any more documents that I might have missed.

I was utterly convinced that the papers I had found were the ones that we had been so desperately searching for. My search revealed nothing else of interest, and so, very much satisfied, Bradley and I left the apartment and once again emerged into the hubbub of the city. I felt that a celebratory drink was very much in order, and we settled down in the first tavern we found and ordered some of the local speciality, an aniseed-tasting drink called raki. I can't say I particularly fell for it, and after my first glass I returned to wine, ordering a carafe, although Bradley seemed to have developed a taste for the cloudy liquid, ordering another glass.

We were out in the afternoon sun for quite some time, watching the ebb and flow of humanity as it drifted all around us, heading to and fro, people bustling through the streets of the city on their trivial matters. We were smug and secure in our knowledge that on my lap were the secrets that would protect Britain from the malice of the Ottoman government. After refreshing ourselves, I decided that it was time to make our news known to the authorities, and so I roused Bradley from his reverie opposite me and we set off for the British Embassy, across the bridge on the opposite peninsula.

It was a modest building, set back from the road in moderately sized grounds. I had decided to return to our inn first and change into my uniform, and so it was that in a red coat and white breeches I was challenged by the similarly dressed guards surrounding the gate. I was taken into the house, and after revealing what I had in my wallet, was granted an immediate audience with the Ambassador to Constantinople, Stratford Canning, the relatively recently appointed 1st Viscount de Redcliffe.

We were ushered in by various aides and attendants and were greeted by a serious-looking man sporting an impressive set of whiskers, who shook my hand firmly and bade me be seated. Bradley remained outside, and was taken off to be given a drink by one of the many plenipotentiaries that were clustered around the place.

'Well, Simms?' he thundered. 'What's this I hear about these papers? A very delicate matter, I understand. Let's hear it, then.' He remained standing and strode around his office, all the while fixing me with his steely gaze.

'Well, Your Lordship, I have reason to believe that I have come across the very documents that I have been sent from England to retrieve; documents that two men have died for already.'

'Upon my soul! Two men, dead! Who?'

'Burnes, of the Foreign Office, and Nikolai Lyubomir, an Ottoman agent masquerading as a Greek Orthodox priest in the service of King Otto. Burnes was hanged by Turkish assassins, while Lyubomir died trying to murder me.'

'Trying to murder you! Good Lord! What has the world come to? Englishmen attacked by Turks and Bulgarians dressed as Greeks. Utterly mad.'

'Quite, My Lord. Anyhow, I believe that I have brought with me these infamous papers, outlining the Turks' plans for the Crimea.'

'Yes, yes. Well, get them out.'

I pulled the documents from their leather wallet and handed them to him. He studied them for a few minutes before reaching for a bell rope next to his desk, which he sharply tugged. We sat in silence for a minute or two until an out of breath servant tumbled through the doors. Canning looked up and addressed the man, sending him away with, 'Fetch an interpreter if you would be so good, George.'

After the disappearance of George another few minutes passed as the viscount seated himself and perused some papers, leaving me to ponder over matters alone.

Once again the double doors swung open and a small rabbit-like fellow was ushered in; a young aide obviously a bit fresh behind the ears and new from home to these parts. 'You requested my services, sir?'

'Ah! Good. Alberston, isn't it?' The boy nodded his consent to this speculation. 'Take a seat. Now, you know Turkish and can read Arabic script, can you not?' Once again there was a brief nod as he seated himself in front of the desk. 'See what you make of this.' Canning handed him the papers and sat back down to await the results.

After several minutes involving the taking out of a notepad and some fervent scribbling from the young man, he had an answer for us.

'Er, well, sir, it appears to be a series of orders for... an Ottoman assault upon our troops in the Crimea!' he said with a tone of slight disbelief.

Canning raised himself from his seat. 'It is as we thought then, Simms. A terrible business indeed. Well, we must notify Raglan and the rest of the commanders. Prepare a messenger to set out for Sevastopol.'

I was amazed to hear this. I had always pictured myself triumphantly presenting the British generals with the documents, and being hailed as a mighty victor. I'd be damned if some wet-around-the-ears aide-de-camp was going to steal my thunder.

'If I may, sir, I feel that delivery of the papers should be entrusted to someone who can be fully trusted and understands completely the importance of this whole affair.'

'Hmm... and who might you suggest, Simms?'

'Well, sir, none other than myself. I've come all the way from London to safeguard these papers and I'd rather not surrender my duties just yet. Allow me to carry them across the sea and notify Raglan, and then rejoin my regiment there. If I don't go now, then I'll have to come all the way back again in a month. If you'll allow young Albertson to transcribe the orders into English then we can be off. I'll be there in a week, and we can prepare for the Turkish attack.'

Canning stood silent and frowned deeply. For several minutes he remained with his back to us, facing out of the window over the city, deep in thought, until at last he turned again.

'Alberston, if you would be so good, translate the Turkish papers into English for Captain Simms. Captain, I do believe that you have a passage to Sevastopol to secure. I'll send a runner down to your lodgings with the papers tonight; by tomorrow morning I expect you to be gone.'

'Thank you, sir, and goodbye.'

'Godspeed, Simms.'

I strode out of the room with grim satisfaction, and giving the name of our inn to an attendant, made my way downstairs to wait while Bradley was fetched. In the meantime I indulged myself by having a fortifying cigar out in the sunshine.

I must say that Bradley wasn't best pleased when I told him of my intentions, and he grumbled considerably the whole way back to the tavern. It wasn't difficult to secure passage to the Crimea, and for a reasonable price I was able to barter our journey to Sevastopol off a grizzled old captain who was due to leave with a cargo of linen for the port later that night.

We enjoyed a leisurely dinner of spiced lamb stew and a few glasses of the local raki, until Canning's courier arrived with the English copy of the papers as well as the original documents. After his departure, we packed up the little that we had brought and made our way down to the docks, where we boarded the ship and deposited our belongings in our cabin before taking a stroll around the deck and watching the men load up the bundles of cloth for sale in the markets of the Crimea – or more likely for sale to the quartermasters of the French and British armies.

It was shortly before nine o'clock when the ship was ready to sail, and as we cast off for the Black Sea it was quite peaceful watching the sun set behind the retreating city, bathing the whole of Constantinople in vivid reds and oranges before dusk took hold, darkness fell and we retired to our cabin.

Part Three
The Crimea

Chapter Twelve

The journey east was no more comfortable than the last one, except for the fact that the ship was even more of a rat-ridden old tub than the last vessel had been. The voyage was not enjoyable, the food being hard and stale, but at least this ship kept a supply of grog on board, which helped the days pass by.

Bradley and I seemed to be the only English-speaking souls on board, the rest of the crew either being Turkish or Bulgarian, but with the employment of a pack of cards and a chess set we had brought from Venice we were able to while away the time without too much boredom. It was so frustrating, as for the last week or so everything had been a hectic chase, rushing through the streets of Venice, and then Constantinople, and the blur of events culminating in the death of Brivopolis and our search of his dingy rooms and securing the papers for England. Now we were slowly drifting across the Black Sea, on a pathetic wind, and were powerless to increase our speed, no matter how hard we wished for it. Every day that we delayed floating around was another day lost in preparing against the Turkish attack on the Crimea. If Alberston had read correctly, then the Turkish attack was scheduled to commence in seven days' time, and troops all along the peninsula were moving to their allotted places to prepare to drive their allies back to the shore and away to the west, leaving them and the Russians to grind it out over the sludge of Balaklava and Sevastopol.

Personally I could see no logic in the treachery of the Ottomans. Why strike now, when the Russians were still a threat, and the allies were so firmly entrenched and prepared for war? Why not wait till the Russians were a distant and weakened menace and the allies had grown soft, believing the war to be almost over and preparing to leave for home? I saw no reason why Britain and France could wish to add the muddy rock that was the Crimea to either of their empires, or go to so much bother about it. Bradley and I discussed this point at length over a game of chess, and he offered the opinion that perhaps the Turks were basing their presumptions on astronomy, or the words of their augurs, as 'they still hold with such nonsense, not like a British government would'. This was the sound judgement of Bradley, and he stuck to this, convinced of the pagan influences in operation in the Sultan's Court. This was how we passed our time, speculating on the finer aspects of the Russian campaign, and waiting while we drew closer each day to completing our mission.

Chapter Thirteen

It was with joy that I finally heard one of the crew remark that we were getting close to our destination. Indeed, I could now see the peninsula on the horizon, a dark mass huddling at the bottom of an empty sky, and pointed this out excitedly to Bradley, who was equally delighted to learn that our voyage would soon be at an end. I was able to discern that we would arrive later that night from the babble of one of the Turkish crew, and headed off back to our cabin to pack up my belongings and to prepare to disembark.

Several long hours passed until we could make out features on the shore. It was a desolate country, bleak with dark pine forests hugging the rocky ground, and the odd serf's hut breaking the emptiness here and there. It transpired that we were to head for Balaklava, the port near the site of that infamous battle. It was a miserable little place, dominated by the Genoese fortress that looked down on the fjord. Really it was just a collection of tents, huts and the odd permanent structure; this was the principal port for the French and British besiegers. A few vessels clustered around at the end of the narrow valley beside a grim-looking collection of buildings which served as storehouses. Redcoats and dock hands were engaged in unloading and transporting the supplies away from the ships, but apart from them the village was virtually deserted. All around us hills loomed up, funnelling the whole focus of the valley northwards, from where we could faintly hear the pounding of guns, although we were at a loss as to whose they were.

We disembarked with little trouble, and leaving Bradley to organise the luggage, I set off to find the duty officer. Given half an hour, some smooth talking, much parading of official letters from both Viscount de Redcliffe and the Foreign Minister, I was able to get two reasonable horses and a guide to take me to the front and the British command. I had asked if they could send a telegraph to the front, but I was told curtly that the lines were once again down. I would have to ride to the front if I wanted to deliver my message.

By this point Bradley had completed overseeing the unloading of our belongings and had stowed them away in a secure place, and we set off with our guide – a young aide-de-camp by the name of Salvesen – leaving the surly corporal in charge to grumble to himself.

The journey to the front was not a pleasant one. The road we took led us to Spring Hill, sight of the British military hospital where Miss Nightingale had done such splendid work. We stopped briefly, as a ranker hobbled past, his leg missing, and the stump a mashed lump of bloody bandage and raw flesh, as he made his way inside. Another hundred yards' ride revealed a soldier emptying the amputated limbs of wounded men into a shallow pit, the stench wafting up towards us. The contrast was chilling. To my left, Bradley was vomiting over the side of his mount while to my right Salvesen, despite being younger, ignored the horror impassively. He had seen this all before, and after all, this was but a taster for what was to come.

After another twenty minutes or so of riding, Sevastopol came into view. It was hard to imagine a more miserable place on earth. The city had yet to fall, and the town had been ripped apart by the constant bombardment of the last few years, its great walls shattered and lying in ruins, and many of the houses inside in a state of dangerous disrepair. A grim atmosphere hung over the city while a blanket of grey cloud shrouded the place, giving it a thoroughly depressing feel. From the looks of things, it would not be long until the city fell, for the harbour was filled with British and French ships, and below us hundreds of guns poured fire onto the beleaguered port. I cannot say that I envied the Russian troops stuck in the fortified city, for although their supply lines were not yet cut, the position they were defending was nothing more than a pile of rubble plagued with disease and death from the ever-active allied guns.

Suddenly a troop of cavalrymen stormed up the hill and drew themselves to a halt at our side. They wore the blue jackets and striped knickerbockers of the 'Death and Glory boys' or the 17th

Lancers, the Duke of Cambridge's regiment. I have to admit I was amazed to see that the regiment was still around, for the reports coming home had declared the regiment almost annihilated by Cardigan's foolery at Balaklava in October last year. Their leader introduced himself as Sergeant Peter Woodcock, and declared that these thirty-eight men were all that were left of the regiment and had been attached to the British command as a reconnaissance company, whose job it was to scout out the terrain east of Sevastopol, where the Russian raiding parties attempted to outflank the armies of the entente, and the Ottoman forces had been given the task of countering their efforts. He announced that he and his troop were heading back to Raglan with details of their mission. He revealed that things had seemed odd in the east. He had seen few Turkish troops manning the lines, indeed the whole land had seemed empty, with neither Ottoman nor Russian to be seen. He condescended to join us and so we set off again on our journey down the hill towards the mess of Sevastopol.

It turned out that Raglan was to be found on the western side of the city overseeing the preparation for yet another assault on the ramparts. What we could hear now was the artillery barrage that was to soften up the Russians before the first wave heaved themselves out of the siege lines and rushed up to the breach that would hopefully be made; indeed we could see columns of infantry making their way from the rear to the front.

As we continued on our journey the landscape began to grow more and more desolate, and the flow of wounded increased, dragging me back to the reports that I had read in *The Times* and making them all the more vivid and horrific now that I was able to visualise them at first hand.

Soon more troops appeared on the northwards road to swell our ranks, notably the Scots Guards, who trudged miserably alongside us, kilts swaying while one of their number mournfully sang a dirge, the words of which floated across the columns of marching men towards us, giving the whole march the feel of a funeral procession. Before long I caught sight of my regiment, the 'Old Buffs', and there was a great degree of handshaking with the fellow officers and men whom I had become acquainted with, which brought some jollity to the affair. However, I was disappointed to hear that some of the chaps who had left Plymouth would not be coming back, most notably Harry de Vere, a lieutenant with whom I had enjoyed a good many nights of revelry in the officers' mess. I had a brief moment of silence for the old boy before we resumed our search for Raglan.

Before long Salvesen trotted up and informed me that we had almost reached Raglan's reported position, and so, after wishing the Buffs well, I summoned Bradley and Woodcock and we cantered off after Salvesen up a dirt track that led off the main road and up to a nearby ridge. After ten minutes of good riding, a cluster of white tents came into view, with a great many men milling to and fro. We approached the encampment and dismounted, allowing our horses to be led off by an eager young aide-de-camp, and inquired after Lord Raglan. We were met by an uppity young captain (who had quite clearly bought his commission, for he had no respect for his betters), who haughtily inquired who we were and what our business was. Of course I straightened my back at this, and putting on my most condescending tone declared that I, Captain the Honourable Henry Simms, was here at the express behest of Lord Canning, Viscount de Redcliffe and the Foreign Minister, and was bearing documents that were crucial for the outcome of the war and urgently required His Lordship's perusal.

This cowed the young buck slightly, and, at a loss for a suitably peevish comment, he agreed to lead us to the general, but warning us that we were not guaranteed an audience, due to the intricate planning of this fresh offensive, of which Raglan and his accomplice, Lord Cardigan, were the sole pioneers. (No surprise there, I noted wryly. Who better to send men on a death or glory charge than Brudenell? Every army needs its own deluded fool, and he was exclusively ours.)

We were ushered into the largest of the canvas tents which were huddled on the ridge, and were told to wait quietly while our man spoke to His Lordship. After a minute or two he re-emerged, and silently gestured for us to go in, announcing me as I entered a room full of middle-aged gentlemen, most of whom were clustered around a camp table and a map in the centre of the tent.

Raglan himself was at the far side of the table and rose upon our entry. He was a sturdy-looking man, and although he looked weary he spoke bombastically, asking angrily, 'And who may you be, pray?'

I had been preparing myself for this moment, for I heard that Raglan was a stubborn fool, and I would require a spectacular first impression to win him over to my side.

'I, sir, am Captain Henry Simms, of the Buffs, although I am not currently serving with them—'

'Then why the devil are you here, sir?' he interrupted. 'What possible desire would you have to travel to this accursed land without an order to do so?'

'Orders I do have, sir, of a kind. My arrival here is an extended conclusion of some business the Foreign Minister has employed me to do on his behalf.'

'Oh, really? Well, what is your business, O lackey of Westminster?'

'I have here for you some documents of a most shocking nature, which I implore you act upon immediately. In this satchel are the Turkish originals, and a translation into English prepared by Viscount de Redcliffe's aide for your immediate attention.'

I handed him the satchel, which he opened suspiciously, and drew forth the papers that had caused so much trouble. He sat down on a nearby campaign chair and began to read, his eyes slowly growing more and more astonished as he absorbed each line.

The atmosphere inside was tense now; everyone had stopped their business and was silent, waiting for the baron's next move. Finally, he spoke.

'May I ask, sir, where you obtained these documents? You must realise that these papers are declaring something which is quite impossible. The Ottomans are our allies, you know?'

Of course I bloody knew. The man was treating me like a damn fool. Was he always this naive? Restraining my frustration, I explained to him a summarised version of events, all the way through which he did nothing except twiddle his whiskers in a most irritating way.

'And do you have any official backing to these wild claims of treachery?' he asked, scrutinising me with a steely gaze.

'I do, sir,' I replied, and fished out my letters of authenticity from London and Canning, and handed them to him. These two were subject to his scrutiny. All the while no one moved or spoke.

After reading these new documents he let out a great sigh and turned to speak to the room.

'Gentlemen, what I have just read is a list of orders outlining an Ottoman attack upon French and British positions in an act of base treachery.'

The declaration had the effect that I had expected: gasps and open eyes all round.

Raglan continued, booming each word out in a mocking and theatrical way, making the whole thing sound even more ridiculous.

'I'll hand around the documents for your personal attention, but what course do you recommend, sirs?'

This was the last straw; the course was obvious. I had to speak.

'Sir! If you don't mind me interrupting, I would have to suggest that you must warn the French immediately and move troops to counter the attack at once.'

Instantly the tent fell silent and Raglan turned to glare at me, and, after taking several deep breaths, pompously announced, 'I "must" do this, must I? We still have no direct proof that there will be an attack, and unless I am very much mistaken you wear the uniform of a captain, do you not, Captain Simms? And since when did captains give generals orders, I wonder? Eh?'

Since generals started being obstinate, bloody idiots, I thought to myself, luckily holding my tongue and giving a more civil reply.

'Sir, these letters have been proved to be authentic by the Foreign Minister himself as well as the British Ambassador to the Sublime Porte.[13] On top of that I think you'll find that the report from Sergeant Woodcock's recent scouting trip will hint at unnatural behaviour in the east and a considerable deficit of

---

[13] The Sublime Porte was the gate of the Grand Vizier's apartments at Topkapi Palace in Constantinople, where the Sultan traditionally received foreign ambassadors. It grew to mean to the Ottoman Empire's foreign ministry.

Ottoman troops manning the front lines. Sir, we have here documents that give us details, directions, times, dates, locations, regiment listings, even the order of march and order in the line of the Ottoman Army for the scheduled attack – which, if I may add, has been ordered for tomorrow. If you have any desire to stay in the Crimea, and have an army to return to Britain at the head of, then you will take heed of this gift that has fallen into our hands.'

A stunned and outraged Raglan stared at me in amazement before slowly declaring, 'You, sir, are an impudent young pup! An outspoken, out of line, pup! I suppose I can do nothing but concede to your demands, seeing as you have such high powers supporting you, but I'm telling you one thing: the attack on Sevastopol continues!'

'Sir, do you not think that a little unwise, to force your army into fighting on two fronts?' I inquired. 'Surely that will lessen our chances of winning in both conflicts.'

'*Nonsense!* That attack goes ahead. The French can hold off the Ottomans to the east, I'll send them a few regiments to help, but apart from that the attack will commence tomorrow morning at eight o'clock.'

I groaned. Eight was the appointed hour for the Ottoman assault. All around the city, British troops would wake up and be ordered to begin the attack on the Russians, and then, to the east, the French troops would be suddenly overcome by thousands of Ottomans, streaming over the ridges and down towards the city, sweeping the allied troops back to the shore, where they would be trapped.

No matter how hard I pleaded, Raglan was not to be moved; the assault would continue as planned, and a small detachment would be sent east to buoy up the French, who would be warned. I was in some doubt as to how well informed the French commanders would be. Would Raglan send them copies of the papers and explain the Ottoman movements, or would he simply give them a brief, cursory overview, telling them to be wary of a petty raid from the Turks, dismissing my information as a wild rumour? I highly suspected that the latter option would be the case…

I was in doubt about how to act next. What should I do now?

Go home? I was at a loss. I was not formally attached to my regiment, or any unit, but I knew I would feel rather useless if everyone else was fighting for their lives and I was sitting snug, safe and sound back in Balaklava while the casualties poured into Spring Hill. I decided to find myself a commission with a regiment in need of a spare captain, and so after being directed to the staff officer, a Major Whitby, I was assigned to command a company of the Rifles, who were to join the line as part of a mixed battalion which would follow the Forlorn Hope into Sevastopol. Their objective was to act as skirmishers around the ramparts and then clear the walls of defenders.

I was ordered up to the Redan, where the Russians had held an outpost for many months, but which had been recently captured by the British. It was a mess of a place, piles of wood, sandbags and spiked cannons everywhere, as well as the general debris that accompanies military outposts under siege. To the east lay several more hilltop forts, and the Russian trenches. To the north lay Sevastopol, huddled around the port, looking grey and uninviting in the pale afternoon sun that filtered down through the thick and dull smog. Engineers had partially reconstructed the ramparts since their destruction a few days ago, and a few cannons had been set up in the centre of the fort. It would be from here that the columns would pour down into the valley, with the Forlorn Hope going first,[14] flanked by the skirmishers that my company were part of; their job was to protect the Forlorn Hope as they sprinted towards the breach that our guns had made.

It wasn't hard to find my new command; the fort was small and their uniforms were distinctive. The company sat in a corner, huddled around a few small fires, their famous green jackets bringing a splash of colour to the otherwise dull grey surrounding. All around them lay the wreckage of war, with splintered gun carriages, rubble and sandbags strewn around where the Russians had abandoned them. The men themselves were surly, unshaven with bags under their eyes, and glared at me as I approached.

---

[14] The Forlorn Hope (Dutch, *verloren hoop*, meaning 'lost troop') was the first unit through the breach. Made up of loose men and led usually by a junior officer, it offered a chance to gain instant promotion, for survivors were rare; but many men were prepared to take the risk for the enticing rewards on offer.

However, for all their unkempt appearance I noticed the weapons from which the regiment got their name were in impeccable order, their barrels gleaming from dedicated polishing. I had been given the name of their senior officer, a Lieutenant Derriman, and I called out for him.

All eyes were suddenly fixed on me, and slowly at the back of the group a long-limbed man unfolded himself and strode towards me. He was young (his attempts at growing a set of mustachios were pitiful) but his eyes, which seemed to belong to an older man, were deep, penetrating and grey, and his face seemed haggard, his hair already thin and receding, accentuating his high forehead. Removing a long, thin cheroot from his mouth he extended a hand, and in a vice-like grip, shook mine.

'Captain Simms, of the Buffs, and this is Sergeant Bradley,' I said, gesturing to Bradley at my side.

'Lieutenant Derriman, the Rifles.'

I detected more than a slight tone of arrogance and pride as the man announced himself; the Rifles were infamous for being disrespectful and unruly – they did not take well to outside officers. I continued, determined to stamp my authority from the start.

'I've been assigned by Major Whitby to command this company during the assault. I assume you're aware of our orders?'

The man's surprise was evident, and his face took a more hostile and wary expression; obviously he had been in command here for quite some time, and I doubted he would willingly surrender his role easily.

'I was not aware of our orders for tomorrow… *sir.*' He lingered sardonically on the last word. 'My orders at present are for the company to hold this position until further notice.'

'Well, I'm giving you further notice, Lieutenant. The Rifles will act as part of a skirmishing half-battalion made up of loose companies. We are to guard the Forlorn Hope and the supporting regiments of the line from possible Russian counter-assaults. I intend to inspect your men in five minutes.'

I motioned to Bradley to join me as I lit up a cigar, and we turned and marched off leaving a dumbstruck and appalled Lieutenant Derriman frozen to the spot.

Seeing he had yet to move, I turned, and to add insult to injury declared, 'Well, jump to it, Lieutenant! I haven't got all day, you know.'

Glaring at me, the enraged Derriman turned and strode off back to his men and began to rouse them, after each command shooting a withering glance at me. I smiled with grim satisfaction.

Waiting five minutes I waited until the Rifles had formed a line behind me, standing to attention, weapons at their sides.

'George, if you would be so kind?'

Bradley turned on the spot and, marching towards the ranks of men, came to a halt. As he bellowed out a series of commands, the Rifles made their namesakes ready for inspection and stood motionless while Lieutenant Derriman lazily strolled up to me and invited me to inspect his men.

I marched over and, with Derriman in tow, I made my way along the line, while behind me Bradley tutted and sighed at the state of the men's uniform; although I have to admit I was impressed by the way the men carried themselves and cared for their weapons. However, everything that was not involved in firing a gun was a mess. Their crossbelts were dirty, their boots scuffed and in disrepair, the buttons on their uniforms dull and mucky.

Reaching the end of the line, I spun around and strode back to the centre and, facing the men, began to talk.

'Well, your uniforms are a mess, your kit dirty and grimy and your appearance unkempt. However, to give you credit, you are obviously proud of your weapons, and you seem to be good soldiers. I am Captain Simms, and will be commanding you tomorrow as you protect the Forlorn Hope. Obey my orders, follow me and fight bravely, and the rewards will be great. I'll see to it that every man gets twice his share of drink and extra rations. Be disrespectful, and I'll make sure that you spend the next six months of your lives polishing your boots to get rid of the last six months' worth of muck! Lieutenant Derriman, I expect every man here to do his duty to his best capacity, and you to ensure this. Can I rely on you?'

The man pondered for a few seconds, and giving a last decisive look at his men, looked me in the eye, nodded and extended his hand once again, this time his grip softer, 'Yes, sir, you can.'

'Right, men. Get a good night's rest. I expect to see you all at half past six tomorrow morning on parade, ready for the attack, with all your kit deposited and only what you'll need for the battle. Goodnight, gentlemen. Lieutenant Derriman, will you join me for a drink and help me find somewhere to sleep?'

Derriman found a room next to his in the ruins of a guard-house in the fort. It was one of the few intact rooms left, and had a bare bedstead leaning rather haphazardly in the corner, but it would do for one night. I got the man talking over a hipflask of Scotch I had brought with me and we shared a couple of cigars, he smoking his long, thin French creations while I preferred a chunkier, more robust cheroot from the Indies, and we discussed the war at length.

The Green Jackets had been here for around four months, and had been mainly used as a picket regiment, running ahead of the lines, skirmishing with Russian cavalry patrols and forage parties, but had only been involved in one major confrontation: the capture of the Redan and the other forts surrounding the city a few days ago. Derriman, along with most of the officers I had met, held the opinion that this assault would be the one that would break Sevastopol. The city was running low on food and water was scare, and now the outer defences had been abandoned, the last line before the city itself was gone. All that protected the town now were crumbling walls, in which British and French artillery had punched several gaping breaches at regular intervals. We passed the time this way for a couple of hours before checking on the men once more and then heading to bed to get an early night to prepare for the trials of the day to come.

Chapter Fourteen

I was woken by Bradley, who informed me that it was six o'clock. Dull grey light filtered through the doorway, and outside a watery sun lit up the desolate scene of the Redan. The Rifles were preparing themselves all around me, buckling on belts, cartridges and other parts of their equipment, while others were making last minute checks on their weapons. Another twenty minutes later, and the company was assembled on parade ready for inspection. I let Derriman speak to them, giving them an inspiring speech, reinforcing the importance of their task, for if they failed, then the Forlorn Hope would be dead before they even reached the breach – a poor result if anything – and this would in turn spell disaster for the whole army, who would be left exposed to Russian cavalry charges and possibly a sally forth from the town.

The guns had fallen silent now. I gave orders for the Rifles to assemble in marching order at the gate. Our numbers were swelled by the ranks of the Forlorn Hope, who had joined us earlier that morning, and who assembled behind us in the order of march. Behind them came the 1st Battalion of the Coldstream Guards, packing the hilltop fort further. At locations all along the lines to the east and west we could see similar parties assembling, all eagerly waiting for the signal.

At half past six exactly the signal came, a single, booming cannon shot, which echoed all around the silent valleys and ridges. Behind me a flare came streaming up from the Redan, an indication that we had received the message. The major of the Coldstream Guards nodded to the Captain of the Forlorn Hope, and in a thin, wavering voice cried, 'Forlorn Hope, the Rifles and the Guards, prepare to advance. Forward march!'

Behind me the pipes of the Guards struck up a jolly tune, 'The Green Hills of Tyrol', which quickened the step of the troops, and we proceeded down the hill towards the ruins of Sevastopol. Our assault was to be covered by final few rounds from the batteries to the rear, and as we marched downhill the roar of dozens of guns begun, shells whizzing over our heads and crashing into the rooftops of the town. When we had marched 200 yards or so I ordered the Rifles to move into skirmish formation, and they darted off, forming a net of Green Jackets around the Forlorn Hope, who stayed in marching column. So far we were yet to be challenged, but I had given orders for the company to fire at will. The barrage from behind continued until we were about 500 yards from the walls, which seemed to be a lot more substantial than they had from the safe and distant Redan. Suddenly the guns fell silent and the Rifles stole forward, running swiftly, darting in and out of the undergrowth until they were in range.

'Rifles! Clear the ramparts! Give our boys a chance!' I bellowed, and as one the companies' weapons turned and began to take pot shots at the Russian defenders, now fully visible on the walls. They returned fire, but fell in far larger numbers than the widely spaced Green Jackets. I could hear the duty officer behind me yell, '*Forlorn Hope, quick march!*' and let out a high-pitched scream on his whistle.

The red-coated men sped past, bearing ladders and muskets, and rushed towards the ramp of rubble that formed the breach. To the east and west I could see red and blue-coated troops doing the same, some already scaling the pile of ruins and into the smoke of the breach.

The Forlorn Hope streamed up to the walls and poured into the hole. Almost immediately five of their men were thrown back in a mist of blood as a Russian volley caught them at the pinnacle of the ramp. Five more redcoats rushed forward to take their place and soon they too fell, lost to our eyes in a smog of thick and rancid powder smoke.

Our job was done, and it was time to return to the Guards, who were preparing to follow the Hope, waiting for the signal.

'Rifles! To me, fall back to the Guards!'

I sped back, turning every few paces to check the progress of my company. There were a few men with light wounds, and I had seen a couple go down, but apart from that they seemed unscathed. Looking back towards the hills I saw the ridges heaving with columns of red and blue uniformed troops, pouring down towards the city. Inside the walls the roar of cannon opened up, hurling deadly missiles towards the advancing armies, throwing up sprays of earth around the columns of men.

At last I caught sight of the one of the Forlorn Hope, standing at the crown of the breach, wildly waving the red, white and blue of the Union Jack. Behind me I heard the order come, 'Coldstream Guards, fix bayonets! By the right, quick march!' Once again the pipes struck up, accompanied by the heavy tramp of the battalion's boots as the troops surged forward.

As he passed, the major turned to me. 'Will you join us, Captain? We're in the walls, come, enjoy the prize!'

I was unsure, for what if the Ottomans were to attack? But Raglan had given his word, and had said troops in the east were watching out. What harm could come of it? Surely there would be a greater chance of victory if we seized Sevastopol anyway? Looking around, I saw that my men were eager, hungry to enjoy the spoils of the fallen city. Reaching a decision, I turned, and nodded.

'The Rifles will advance on my command. Quick march!' Once again the Green Jackets stole forward towards the breach, following in the wake of the 1st Battalion. Most of the troops were over the ramp and were plunging into the narrow corridor ahead. Striding up the rubble I reached the crest, and raising my sword, checked behind me for the rest of my men. Beneath me was a sea of redcoats, bunched up, trapped by the thick walls of the surrounding houses.

Suddenly the entire scene erupted in a hell of smoke and fire. All around me piles of rubble were thrown up into the air. I was tossed back, and sent careering down the slope I had just climbed. I lay half-buried under the debris, stunned by the force of the explosion. There was only one answer – the Russians had mined the breach. Anticipating that the narrow passage beyond would be crowded with British troops, they had packed the surrounding houses full of explosives and set them off, decimating the invading ranks.

I staggered to my feet, and surveying the horrific scene before me through dazed eyes. In the alley before me lay hundreds of moaning, heaving and bloody men, many lacking limbs, while their dead comrades lay all around them. Feeling sick, I stumbled back down the ramp, tripping over bodies and stones, covered in dust and blood. Falling over once again, my hands grasped a staff, or some other piece of equipment, and using this I was able to hobble off. At my feet some of the Green Jackets were heaving themselves up, equally stunned expressions of shock and horror frozen on their faces.

'Green Jackets! To me! To me!'

I had reached the foot of the breach, back outside the walls now. More of my men had survived than I had thought. I was pleased to see Bradley appear at my side, even though he looked awful, cradling a bloody arm. Turning to the east, I saw the armies of the French and British storming towards me. Turning to the north, I saw something that chilled me to the very bone.

A Russian counter-attack. And in their trail, the army of the Ottomans. How foolish we had been to assume the weakest power here would try to land the biggest punch! For reasons unknown, the Turks and Russians had joined forces, with the sole aim of sweeping the Western powers from the Crimea.

Casting my eye back to the breach, I saw that more redcoats had survived than I had thought. I heard the major rallying his men, calling for them to press on into the city. I was unsure whether ours was the only breach to have been detonated or whether the same fate had befallen all three of the entry parties. Rushing back up the breach, I saw the Guards and what was left of the Hope hurrying off into the town, eager to wreak their vengeance. A lone piper was raising his instrument and stirring their hearts with a rousing, wailing tune. Turning back to face the friendly forces to the south, I realised immediately that they were too far away, unable to defend the breach. If we left, the Ottomans would enter the city and flush out our troops, ending any chance of us ever crushing the newly revealed alliance. It was up to the Rifles, a handful of redcoats, and me (of all people, to have such cursed luck!) to hold this bloody heap of rock.

'Rifles, to me!'

The Green Jackets scrambled up, hauling themselves up the ramp.

'Take positions around the breach – we must hold it! If we fail, any troops left in the city will die…' I noticed all the men were gazing up, above my head. Raising my gaze, I saw that the staff I had grabbed in my haste to scramble away was nothing less than the colours of Forlorn Hope. Above me, the Jack had fully unfurled, gloriously spilling out and streaming behind me, the red, white and blue crosses forming a vivid splash of colour against the drab grey of the ruins.

'Men, we have little or no chance of holding the breach for long, but if we can, then we can buy the army time to save the advance parties and secure a victory, bringing an end to this muddy hell. Take up your places, ready your guns. We take not a step back!'

The Rifles ensconced themselves among the rubble, and raising their weapons prepared to face the rapidly advancing enemy. The haze of men and horses were now little more than 500 yards away, and gaining. Our troops were almost a mile away; we were alone in this fight. Raising the colours defiantly, I called out in what I hoped was a rousing way, 'Not a step back, lads! This flag does not go down while a Briton still stands!' Now they were less than 400 yards off, and bearing down upon us.

'Company! Present arms!' A group of redcoats had assembled behind me, and Bradley, acting quickly, had organised them into two ranks, and they raised their muskets to prepare for the volley.

'Make ready!' There was a clatter all around as the troops cocked their weapons, priming the firing pan.

Now the enemy were little more than 300 yards away, I could make out details on their uniforms, pick out their faces, the facings on their jackets.

'Take aim!'

200 yards.

150…

100…

'Fire!'

Once again the breach erupted with smoke as the ragged volley sped towards the advancing foe. The front rank of the enemy was cut down, thrown into a bloody swirl by my men. The bulk of their troops were continuing past us, heading for the entente forces, but a considerable detachment – maybe a battalion at most – was assaulting us.

'Reload!'

A flurry behind me as we prepared to fire again. Ahead of me the Russians were presenting their weapons.

'Steady, boys!'

I saw the officer's mouth open and braced myself for the impact of their volley. A fog of wadding and smoke sped toward me. All around me the balls skittered on and chipped the rubble, and judging by the number of cries, quite a few had hit their mark. Luckily, I had escaped unscathed. I could not say the same for the rifleman at my feet, his head thrown backwards, and a bloody hole where his eye had been.

'Company! Take aim! Fire!'

Our second volley was considerably lighter than the first, and I doubted my rapidly depleting force would hold them off for much longer. To the south I could hear the first sounds of conflict between the two opposing armies, little more than 400 yards away. If we could just hold them for a little longer…

The Russian officer in command had obviously decided that now was the time to end this business. His men had fixed bayonets, and were clearly planning to sweep us away with a quick and final assault into the breach. There was still time yet, however, to loose another volley into their packed ranks.

'Company, to me! Form square! Present arms! Hold your fire, wait for my command!'

The Russians began to advance, feet pounding in time to the lone drummer in their midst. Up they came, stumbling up the wreckage of their own walls, eager to end the battle and join their comrades inside the city in repelling the British invader.

They were barely fifty yards away when I bellowed the deadly order. I was lost in powder smoke as the men under my command discharged their rifles and muskets. Thrusting my sword forward, I cried, 'The company will advance! Forward the Rifles!'

As one we rushed down the slope and leapt into the Russian ranks. My sword plunged into the first man I met, a heavily bearded brute. Swinging my weapon wildly all around me, I saw that my men were being forced back, desperately fighting for their lives. In one hand I held the colours, in the other my blade. I cut and slashed at anything within my reach, and in my passion I almost cut down one of my own men, a terrified young redcoat, who did nothing but stare at me, a dusty and bloody apparition bearing down upon him. I checked myself at the last moment, and watched as he was speared on the end of a Russian bayonet, thrust though his ribcage, protruding hideously. I sliced the attacker's face, and both victim and assailant fell to the ground dead. Looking around me wildly, I saw I had less than five or six men left, Bradley battling with a huge bearded sergeant to my right. I sallied forward, eager to help him, only to be struck from behind. All I remember next is falling, as the rubble rushed up to meet me, and hugging the colours close to me while the sound of bugles erupted all around.

Part Four

London

Chapter Fifteen

The sun in Hyde Park was glorious. Utterly glorious. At my side, my fiancée daintily sipped tea, the glorious sun playing on her golden hair. Behind us the riders made their way sedately along Rotten Row, all eager to be seen sporting the latest fashions. On the table before me lay a copy of today's *Times*. Open at the Obituaries page, I examined the article before me.

> The Right Honourable Marcus Oswald Simms, 4th Baron Rigby, MP for Underbourne, Kent, of Oakam House, Oakam, Kent, passed away last week at two o'clock, on Thursday morning, 28th August, 1856. Famous for his work as Ambassador to the Danish Court from 1830–37, he pioneered several trade agreements that secured fresh markets for British wool abroad, and can be held responsible for the friendly relations that these two great countries now share. Baron Rigby, who was seventy-three years old at the time of death, passed on due to natural causes, after having lived a long and fulfilling life. Father of Henry and Richard Simms, and husband of Elizabeth Simms, née Otterly, and upon her death, husband of Camilla Simms, née Drummond, he will commemorated in a service at the church of St Mary at Oakam.

Turning over the page, I came to the announcements and appointments section of the paper. Again I perused the page, glancing down it, and one particular article caught my eye.

> On Wednesday the 3rd September, 1856, at the church of St Mary in Oakam, will be celebrated the marriage of Miss Isabella Burnes and the Hon. Henry Simms, who recently succeeded as the 5th Baron Rigby. All guests are welcome to attend the service, which will take place at eleven o'clock.

I flicked back to the front of the paper, to page five. I was greeted with a pleasing headline – 'Captain the Honourable Henry Simms, hero of Sevastopol' – and beneath it a large column.

Reporting from the Crimea, in the ruins of the fallen city of Sevastopol, Mr James Fulton has uncovered a story of remarkable bravery and heroism from the British troops involved in the capture that infamous place.

Now a major, Captain Henry Simms, of the Royal East Kent Regiment, single-handedly held the breach against a whole battalion of Russian assailants, defiantly holding them with nothing but a handful of men he had assembled from the ruins of the Forlorn Hope. This new hero of Britain bravely assembled his company and, seizing the sacred colours of Britain, held back the Russian foe. Again and again he and his troops pushed back the invader, repelling their countless assaults while British and French forces hurried to relieve their courageous brothers in arms. Seeing that he was almost overwhelmed, the inspirational Major Simms led a death-or-glory charge down the slope, plunging into enemy ranks. Even though his men were cut down around him, Major Simms stayed defiant, and was rendered unconscious while rushing to help of one of his men. He was found, minutes later, by a relieving cavalry charge made by the remnants of 17th Lancers, clutching the blood-soaked colours to his breast while around him his bold men lay, having successfully saved the British assault on the city, and bringing on our swift victory in the Crimea.

It had been a hectic week. I had been back a month, and since that fateful day I was now the 5th Baron Rigby, also known as Major the Lord Rigby, and was soon to be united with my beloved Isabella. Lazily flicking the pages of the paper, one final article caught me eye. Calling Bradley over – he had been obediently standing behind, now back in his capacity as my manservant – I gestured to a cartoon in the centre of the page. It showed two men, one obviously intended to be me (at least our whiskers matched), and the other a young British soldier gesturing off to one side. We were depicted standing victorious on a pile of Russian dead, the Union Jack wrapped around me like a toga. Underneath the illustration lay the cringe-inducing caption: 'I believe you missed one, sir!'

After acknowledging the terrible thing with a chuckle, I ordered Bradley to pack up the things. Tonight we dined at Oakam, and if I was not mistaken, Father had always kept a very, very well-stocked cellar. I came to the conclusion that life could be little better than this, and if it was, well, it was no great loss, particularly when you have a case of eighty-year-old claret lurking around the house somewhere. Life was good.

Lightning Source UK Ltd.
Milton Keynes UK
12 June 2010

155456UK00001BA/3/P